Love is for Life
& Beyond

Love is for Life & Beyond

YASHWANT KANODIA

Srishti
PUBLISHERS & DISTRIBUTORS

SRISHTI PUBLISHERS & DISTRIBUTORS
Registered Office: N-16, C.R. Park
New Delhi – 110 019
Corporate Office: 212A, Peacock Lane
Shahpur Jat, New Delhi – 110 049
editorial@srishtipublishers.com

First published by
Srishti Publishers & Distributors in 2018

10 9 8 7 6 5 4 3 2 1

This is a work of fiction. The characters, places, organisations and events described in this book are either a work of the author's imagination or have been used fictitiously. Any resemblance to people, living or dead, places, events, communities or organisations is purely coincidental.

Printed and bound in India

Acknowledgements

This is my debut novel, and as I transverse my journey from an avid reader to a writer, I would like to express my gratitude towards all the people who have supported and motivated me to write this book by providing their remarks and comments to help me write better.

This book is very close to my heart, and writing this book was not easy. I couldn't express my happiness that I finally made through it. Thanks to my friends and family for talking to me endlessly about this book and encouraging me to write this book in spite of all the cherishable moments I missed spending with them.

My parents, who supported me on every phase of this book and constantly motivated me to pursue my passion.

Most importantly, special thanks to my close friend Riya for her words of assurance and excitement. She is the only person who read this book many more times than I did.

For Varun, my editor: Thanks for all your suggestions and critical remarks that made me a better storyteller.

A lot of gratitude to Malvika for her constant guidance and support by reading the drafts word by word in our favourite café. A special shout out to my two sisters Priyanka and Ankita for backing me up and lifting my confidence even in the middle of the night.

Most importantly, thank you for reading this book. (I hope you like it.)

Om Sai Ram.

Prologue

"Here is your boarding pass, sir. Please proceed towards the immigration," requested the cabin crew at the check-in counter.

Ahh! I heaved a sigh of relief. Exhausted and burned out from the continuous meetings in the last two days, an hour long wait in the queue was just too much for my lethargic body.

I was returning home to Delhi, happy that the convention had gone well in Mumbai. Renaissance Hotel on the banks of Powai Lake will be holding tight in my memory. A shudder ran through my veins. The fact that I was going to soon tell my father about my recent business accomplishments made my chest bloat with pride.

Once on my seat, I closed my eyes stretching my legs forward and gasped the air inside the flight cabin. So fresh and cold it was, that it for a moment reminded me of Shanaya. It rejuvenated my desiccated veins. Four years and counting, I would say that god had been benevolent to me for giving me the love of my life. Even though we had known each other from childhood, our love blossomed when our hormones kicked in. She had been the sturdy pillar of my wavering confidence and always motivated me to enhance my business, although I didn't want to join it in the first place.

Of late, things had been a little scratchy with her. It had been months since we talked properly. Work had been my wicked mistress lately and I was alleged to be the unfaithful one in the relationship.

During the entire flight, a chaotic wave of emotions perturbed me from sleeping after being an owl for almost two days. The bubble of frustration magnifying on her face when I met her the last time flashed repeatedly in front of my eyes, but the trumpet cacophony of this conference's success being the underdog, won the battle. It was the perfect day for me and I was sure that everything would turn out to be awesome.

"We are about to touch Delhi soon; please fasten your seat belts."

In a flash, I opened my eyes. My hands trembled as I checked my seat belt. Only god knew when I would get over with this fear of touchdown, I thought, shaking my head. I looked around and smiled as I was not the only nervous one here. Beside me sat an old man nervously, probably in his sixties. He looked past through me outside the window and closed his eyes shut in the speed of a wink. As the flight took a sharp turn and descended, I turned my head and gazed outside the window. The clouds disappeared and cars as small as in board games came into view along with various houses of different sizes. I felt a sudden bump and frightened, I shut my eyes. As the tires skidded on the tarmac, a puff of air involuntarily gushed out of my mouth.

"Thank god!" I said.

Now that we had landed safely, I couldn't help but daydream how my father would react to my achievements in Mumbai. His gratified face will be a winning trophy for the cocktail of my hard work and sweat. I got up from my seat and walked outside the aircraft towards the belt for luggage. My phone beeped.

"Dad must be waiting," I mumbled grasping my phone from my pocket. My feet stopped when I saw Varun's name flashing on the screen.

"Varun, after a very long time. Let's see how can he add more joy to my day," I croaked as I swiped my finger to the right.

"Hi Varun,"

"Hey, I have to meet you now, it's urgent," he announced haphazardly.

"Umm. I just came back from Mumbai bro, let's catch up tomorrow."

"I won't take no for an answer. I am on the way to your house," he declared clearing his throat.

"Oka..." I stammered as his voice left a staggering thought in my brain. His provocation to meet immediately added a cloud of scepticism in my mind as I rambled towards the exit gate while picking up the luggage.

As I walked out of the exit gate, my eyes got locked on the happy face of my father, which I had never seen before in a decade.

I scuttled towards him as he extended his arms for a hug.

"Welcome back, son. I read the email, Nikhil. You matured the deal with Europe's biggest recycling company. I traced this company for five years, and I never even got a positive response," he blurted while stroking his hand on my back.

"I did it, Dad," I patted myself, being as proud as a daisy.

"I won't deny the fact that my son is doing so much better than me at twenty-three," he whispered in my ear with a smile as wide as an ocean.

"Thanks."

After pulling myself out from the ring of appreciation, I gazed at the people as we walked towards the car. I pulled the door and sat in the backseat of the car with dad. It was midnight, but the airport was populated. On my way back, dad and I discussed what had happened at the convention.

As the driver stopped the car in front of the entrance gate of my bungalow, my phone beeped again. Before moving out of the car,

I hastily pulled the phone from my pocket and saw Shanaya's text which read,

Miss you

My lips stretched into a smile. I opened the car door when I saw my sister Nikita running towards me.

"Joe, I am always there for you and will always love you," she whispered sadly, clutching me tight.

"Let's go inside, sis, Mumma must be waiting," I muttered while walking through the uncomfortable air, wondering what was up with her.

♋

Moments later, I heard the incessant buzz of the doorbell. Annoyed, I opened the door and found a dishevelled Varun standing at the entrance with a sullen look on his face.

He entered quickly, caring not to close the door behind and hugged me.

"Let's go to your room, I have something to tell you," he said catching his breath.

I nodded.

♋

"What happened Varun? You look like shit!" I queried as I sat on my bed, crossing my legs.

"Since the past two days, I have been dying to tell you something. It's killing me," he alleged as he grasped his phone from his pocket. With his eyes dipped in the sea of grief, he repeatedly wiped the sweat on his forehead with the back of his hand.

"Are your parents all right?" I queried with curiosity penetrating my body.

"Yes," he retorted as he rolled his eyes away from me.

"Has anyone died or met with an accident?" I questioned anxiously. The sadness lurking on his face warned me of something ominous coming my way.

"No," he frowned and glanced at me for a brief moment.

Swallowing the saliva in my mouth, I moved closer towards him, "Is it about me?"

He raised his eyebrows, his chest heaved with a sudden sob, and tears shimmered in his eyes, spilling down his cheeks. He inched closer and wrapped his arms around me.

"Nikhil, you are my best friend," he stammered while crying like a two-year-old. "I will be there for you, no matter what happens in life."

"Stop beating around the bush, Varun. First my sister and now you," I blustered pushing him away with my arms and barked. "Just tell me what it is!"

He kept his silence again, dazed, not looking at me. He opened his mouth to say something, but closed it immediately, shaking his head.

Worry sent goose bumps down my back, following the sweat plastering the shirt to my skin. I panicked as vivid thoughts ran in my mind, desperate to unravel the truth. Lightning accompanied by thundering took my eyes away towards the balcony.

"Is it about Shanaya?" I bellowed, astonished to hear my words as they come out of my mouth.

His eyebrows waggled and cheeks flushed as Shanaya's name entered his ears. Like a ghost, he stood still with his arms by his sides.

Picking his shattered existence together, he handed his phone to me with his hands trembling.

"Please read this message, it's too excruciating for me to read it aloud."

Scared, I took his phone and started reading the message. Tears ran down my eyes like a river as I read each word.

I stood still, looking towards the phone which soon fell off from my hand.

"No, no," I muttered shaking my head. "It isn't true."

How I wished it to be false!

My hand closed around my car keys. The pointed edges bit into my skin. At any other time, I would squirm, now I welcomed the pain.

The message was something I wished I had never read.

It was one hell of a frosty December evening. My skin tingled with the cold that seemed everlasting as I walked the streets of New Delhi. The roads were empty; everyone seemed to have rushed to their homes, wanting to avoid the cold. I was only out because I had gone to attend my friend's birthday party. I wouldn't have missed it for any reason.

My inebriated mind failed to register the vibrations of my phone at first, but it caught on fast. The noise was incessant. I got furious and wanted to throw away my phone. I was in no mood to talk, neither to take out my hands jammed in my jacket's pockets. My bones ached and complained, wishing to find the comforts of a bed. Just the thought of bed and cushions sent me into a dream-like slump; only for a moment, though. The cold breeze slapped me awake and brought me back to reality. And also, the vibrations that would never stop. I held the phone tight in my hand, eager to wait for the phone to stop, but then, through the corner of my eyes, I saw a familiar name on the highlighted screen. Shanaya.

I smiled, despite being tired. It was surprising that I could even move those muscles that shaped the curl of my lips. If anyone could do that, it was Shanaya.

Shanaya and I had been friends from kindergarten. We practically learned to speak our first words together. Learning to drink milk from each other's bottles, stealing lunches from other children's bags and what not. Oh, those had been fun times.

As we had grown up, I had seen her evolve, noticed her every trait and change in character. She had now grown up to be a tall girl – quite humorous and optimistic. So much that she had been blessed with an ability to convince you that there was still hope when you lay flat in the darkest dungeons, imprisoned by the cruel demons of your life. I, on the other side, always looked at the glass being half empty. For her, nothing seemed impossible. With excellent grades and a knack for artistic work, I could say that she was a beauty with brains. Her heart was filled with humanity and compassion. She had been a good friend to everybody since childhood, always extending a helping hand to the one in need.

Inhaling an excited puff of air, I slid my fingers to the right of the screen.

"Hi Nikhil," she mumbled.

"Hi Shanaya, how have you been?" I asked with abrupt joy in my heart.

"I am good. What's up with you?"

"Just returning home from Varun's birthday party," I retorted and stopped walking.

"Oh, that's great, and I am sure you must have had fun."

"The party was fantastic and I danced a lot," I exclaimed.

"You did what? Say that again please," she chuckled. Her comment made me laugh from my stomach.

"Don't be so dramatic, Shanaya. I know you heard it, and yes, I can dance, or at least in the dark of night," I simpered though, rather surprised that she still remembered that I couldn't dance.

"Ha-ha, this is the part of you I love," she giggled. Her laugh made my heart melt and I wondered how she did that every time we talked.

"Just my humour?" I asked childishly.

"No, but just everything about you."

"What, really?" My eyes were wide open now.

"I mean... umm..." She paused for a couple of seconds.

I impatiently waited for her to say something – to perhaps say that she was just kidding. But she stayed silent. What did that silence mean? Did this uneasy quiet mean she saw me as something more than... a friend? My excitement did not stop. Neither did the flood of questions in my head.

"Nikhil, I never thought I would, but I want to come out clean and finally tell you what I feel about you," she confessed, her voice frantic.

My hands shook as I stood stunned, holding the phone in my hand. I could not believe what I just heard. No words came out of my mouth.

I glanced down and sat on the footpath. I could feel that there was something vaguely disturbing coming my way.

"I... How should I say it?" she stammered.

I didn't know why, but for the first time in my life, every second felt like a month-long wait. I wished she would say quickly whatever it was she wanted to say.

"I love you, Nikhil." I could hear her take a deep breath.

"I didn't plan to tell you that today, or ever for that matter, as I couldn't get enough courage."

"You love me? But you never said it before?" I asked, my jaws clenched.

"Do you think I am kidding? Don't make me regret it, Nikhil," she muttered.

"Uh, I don't... I don't know what to say, Shanaya," I stammered.

Her words passed through every iota of my body. Dazed by the suddenness of her proposal, I gazed around the street. Suddenly there was some traffic on the road, the honks of the cars were deafening. Beep. Horn. Peep. My body quivering, I stared up into the sky and at the full moon, which seemed to be grinning at me.

"I know you don't like me that way, but today I couldn't control myself. After all, our friendship goes a long way," she continued, her voice trembling.

My heart was agitated with my brows knitted together. My breathing turned heavy, leaving me unable to express myself.

'Cool down, Nikhil,' I told myself.

Ceasing for a moment, I swallowed thickly. "No, I didn't mean that. I really like you, Shanaya, as you are such a good friend of mine…but… this is just out of the blue."

"Nikhil, relax. I am not expecting an answer today." Her voice came in a murmur. "Goodnight."

"I would sleep only if I could, but it seems like a long winter night. Goodnight, Shanaya," I wished her as I press the disconnect button.

A hurricane of thoughts assailed my mind. Somewhere deep inside, I had always known. I had always liked Shanaya. Most of the time, I felt it was because she was a friend. But now… I didn't know what to call our camaraderie. She had confessed that she loved me. Did I love her back? The very question left me vexed. Somewhere in my chest, though, my heart beat as if it was trying to give me an answer. The feeling was ecstatic. I was glad that she had confessed.

I pushed myself up from the ground, dusted my bottom with my hands, and started walking home.

♋

Once in my room, I fell on the bed and tossed around, my mind completely at unrest. My dreams wandered and all I could see in them were Shanaya's hazy brown eyes. I was still trying to comprehend my feelings for her. I couldn't help but wonder. When had she started to like me? She had never shown any feelings. I had always enjoyed her company and never bothered to understand her feelings. The friendship had been just that: a joyous companionship where one understood the other and both had fun.

I woke up twice that night; every time I could hear my heart pounding.

♋

A couple of days passed in vain, leaving me drowning in the river of my thoughts. Was she just my best friend or something more? Did I love her too? I questioned myself repeatedly, but was not sure about my feelings for her.

As I sat in the second last row in my French class during engineering classes in college, while the teacher translated a few of the English words into French, I could not help but daydream about Shanaya.

I pondered about what I would do if I happened to meet her. I wanted to meet her so badly. I turned my head around and glanced towards the back door. It was slightly open. Bending from the top, clandestinely I sprinted out of the class, leaving my friends' mouths wide open.

While congratulating myself for the successful escape, I took out my phone and typed Shanaya's number.

"Hi, what's up?" I asked after she picked. And I bit my teeth soon after. Was this all I could say after the mess that was in my head?

"Um, well, I was in the middle of a movie with my friends," she retorted.

"That's not a problem. I will wait. Call me when you are free please," I requested.

"Sure, I'll call you then," she said and hung up.

I threw up my hands in regret, cursing for not coming to the point in time. I had never been so nervous before in my life while talking to her.

Not able to control my thoughts, I thought of texting her to see if she could meet me that day.

With my body slouched against the wall in the corridor, I opened my message box and started typing. Then I thought about why I needed to make a big deal out of it. Even if she said no, we would still remain friends.

With a heavy and curious heart, I finally sent the message:

Can we meet today?

Within two seconds, I heard my phone's tone, and yes, she had texted back. Phew!

Yeah! Sure, let's meet. Find me outside Select City Walk Mall in Saket.

Goose bumps ran up my skin. Thrilled, I ran towards my car.

On the way, my mind constantly thought about how weird it would be to meet her after the proposal. I prepared myself to face her by cajoling my mind to act normally, just as friends.

Forty-five minutes later, I reached the mall and parked my car. Looking myself up in the rear-view mirror, I straightened my spiky hair.

In the next second, my eyes fell upon Shanaya coming out of the mall. My breaths quickened. She was dressed to kill in her black sweater and blue pants, which complimented her snow-white face. The sunlight falling on her only made her look even more beautiful.

My mouth involuntarily gaped wide open. I had never noticed her like that before.

Until the day before, she had just been a friend. I had never complimented her on her looks. But now, I felt like showering her with praises. Perhaps my feelings were beginning to surface. I snapped my mouth shut. With eyes blinking, I stared at her soft oval face, thick brownish black hair, and a smile on her lips that could make people stop. Hormones rushed inside me. I started thinking about random things. It was all I could do. Our eyes met. I could feel my heart dancing; I smiled like a baby. She looked away, shy and smiling, and then looked again straight into my eyes. She frowned.

Lost in my own euphoria, I didn't notice until she finally pulled my cheek and blurted, "Hi Nikhil."

Earlier, I used to be annoyed whenever she pulled my cheek, but today, I enjoyed the touch of her hand on my face, experiencing an odd exhilarating shiver jolting my spine.

"Hi Shanaya. You look so beautiful today," I complimented, unable to stop myself.

The corners of her lips lifted up and her smile sparkled.

"Thank you. Let's go for a drive," she murmured as she pulled my cheek hard again, and pointed towards the car with her long fingers. Her red nail paint looked exquisitely gorgeous. Still captivated by her smile, I nodded yes.

Later in the car, I grew uneasy with the silence. It felt like someone had just died. I didn't know what to say. The whole camaraderie started to feel weird. Even she looked perplexed, as she ran her hand through her thick, beautiful hair.

"We are still friends, Shanaya. It should not feel so uncomfortable," I shrugged.

"Why did you say that?" she asked, tilting her head to one side, a hint of a smile playing on her lips. "Yes, of course, we are friends. We know each other inside out. How are you anyway?"

"I am fine. Have been twitchy since you called the other day," I said, thinking if she'd got any idea of what's going on in my head.

She huffed, probably feeling the same.

"I am really sorry about that. I didn't mean to come out like this. I was caught in the moment and I spurted out everything at one go," she winced and looked down towards the carpet that dotted the car's floor.

I couldn't have been more pleased.

"So, how're studies?" I asked to digress from the uncomfortable atmosphere.

"B.Com (honours) is tougher than I thought. But I love college life, especially as now I can go out with friends whenever I want till six in the evening. Although I have to bunk classes for that, you know how it is," she chuckled as she threw her hair back from her face.

"No, I don't know," I giggled, just to mess with her. I beheld her face again, and a shiver went down my spine.

"You know my mother has always been strict," she continued.

"I know, and I was just kidding."

"Also, I have my personal phone now, which gives me a little bit of independence and privacy." She went on while I nodded with my mind rambling elsewhere.

All I could hear was the racing heartbeat in my chest. I didn't know why. Never before in my life had I felt so excited about something. I went on nodding my head at her every word. Moments later she announced, "It's time now. Can you drop me to Kamla Nehru College? I have a very important presentation."

Just when I thought we were starting to have a real conversation, she had to go. Damn!

"Sure," I huffed with agitation.

Within fifteen minutes, we reached outside her college. It's always crowded outside the famed convent KNC (Kamla Nehru), just beside Gargi College. With pretty girls coming out and going back in, it was a very desirable place for boys to hang out. Also, many times boys were seen waiting for their girlfriends just outside the college, most dressed up on their fancy bikes and some in their expensive cars.

As I stopped the car on the side, she stepped outside, gazing at me unblinkingly. Although late, I rushed towards her to say goodbye.

Nervously, I moved forward to give her a side hug, but she stretched her arms wide and took me in it rapidly. Her grip tightened up and I could feel the fire lightening in my heart. Sniffing over her ear, I sensed the fragrance of freshly laundered linen and some expensive hair shampoo.

Before this day, I had always heard and read that guys who love their partners love to smell each other's hair. It was the first time I was experiencing that emotion. The fragrance was so intoxicating that for two whole minutes, I inhaled it deep into my lungs in desperation.

Confused, she asked, "Are you okay?"

In response to her question, I pulled myself up just a little. My fingers now ran on her beautiful face, gently examining her. Her face felt as smooth as glass. Then my thumb brushed her upper lip with my eyes staring at her, 'Wow, such pretty lips,' I declared in my mind.

My constant staring held her anxious, burning gaze at the moment, but gradually her shining brown eyes took my mind away. My mind shrieked at me repeatedly to kiss her, but I couldn't move. She exhaled heavily and my breathing almost ceased. Hoping that she would make a move, I shut my eyes, and waited for a couple of seconds. Unfortunately, she stood still, so I immediately pushed back my senses into my brain and opened my eyes. I found her eyes pointed sharply on my lips.

'God! This is going out of limits,' I said in my mouth and drew away from her quickly. She glanced at me once again and turned around and started running towards the dusky corroded gate of her college. 'Wow, that was something!' I cried calming my hormones down and watched her. It would have been funny if she would have turned around just like Kajol did in *Dilwale Dulhaniya Le Jayenge,* but she didn't. My bad luck!

I think anyone could have noticed the disappointment on my face, but her. My Lord! I wanted more.

♋

It had been almost a month now; we had started texting each other daily. Day and night, we exchanged messages. Of course, WhatsApp, like a saviour, saved me a lot of money.

I was really happy with the way things were working out for us. Every day we grew closer to each other, and there wasn't any doubt that my heart started to develop feelings for her. There was something about her that drove me crazy every time. I tried to think hard about what was so special about her that made me so vulnerable and in love. Her beautiful appearance, her humour, her honesty or the way she made me feel.

♋

Many sleepless nights later, I was finally confident that I loved her now. It was just that since the day she confessed, the doors of my heart, which were always closed, had opened. I ended up calling her.

Nervous, I wiped the sweat off my forehead with my hand.

"Hola!" she exclaimed.

"Hi Shanaya! I want to tell you something today."

"Yes, please tell me."

I cleared my throat and took a deep breath. "Shanaya, I love you and I want to be with you. The past two months have been really crazy for me," I admitted.

"Nikhil, I love you too, you know. But last week, Radhika told me that she still loves you and she wants to be with you. I can't tell her that I proposed to you. I don't want to hurt her. She is my friend," she replied.

My mouth twisted. Radhika's name came as a bolt from the blue.

"What? Radhika? I agree that she has been carrying the torch for me since school, but I don't think she really loves me. It's been a couple of months since I have even spoken to her."

"Nikhil, I don't know, it just doesn't seem right."

"Shanaya, if we love each other, then we can tell her that, and if she is really your friend, then I think she will understand."

"I don't know, let me think about it. Please give me some time."

"Call me when you make up your mind then."

What fresh hell is this? Where did Radhika come from all of a sudden? God, if she really doesn't have to do anything with me, then why did she say that she loves me? I thought.

♋

The night was falling and so was the silence. It wasn't long before I started sinking into the cold dark sea. The blackness had abominably affected my hopes. But then, as they say, there is a silver lining to everything. Even though the landscape was far from being fair, I could see a protecting layer of stars in the sky with their heads high in this ocean of darkness illuminating the dark, scary moonless night. I stood rooted to my spot on the balcony outside my room, painting Shanaya's beautiful face between the stars, with my face curving into a smile.

To be honest, I hated the fact that she could mess up my mind so easily. A fire was erupting inside my heart which could only be doused with her presence. Somebody once said to me, "there was a void in my heart which I never knew existed, but had been filled now". I think now I know what he meant. I was sure that she was the one for me and I wanted to give her everything – my heart, body, and soul. I couldn't cope with the feelings of not treating her as a girlfriend anymore. In this roller coaster life, most people often miss the opportunity which could have changed their life. I didn't want to be one of them.

I was already furious from the last time when she, out of the blue, brought Radhika between us. Huh! I was a happy man before she proposed to me, and now she had rejected me. It's like I had no say in the matter. It was painful when I confessed that I loved her and all she had to say was that it didn't feel right.

It was getting tiring being awake like an owl every night thinking about her beautiful smile, her impeccable beauty and the way she made me anxious every time I heard her voice.

My mind implored me not to call her, but my heart – it wouldn't just listen. I snap shut the door of the balcony and came inside my room. My fingers had started dialling her number.

"Shanaya, I cannot take this anymore. I want people to know what I feel for you. I have started to love you now. I want us to be together and if you cannot be with me, it's better that we never talk again," I whined, coming straight to the point.

She started crying and said, "I love you, but Nikhil, what about Radhika?"

"Arghhh! Who is more important – Radhika or me?' I questioned agitatedly.

"If Radhika is really our friend, she will understand that we should be together, and if she doesn't, then it's her problem, not yours. There is no room for guilt in this relationship," I added.

"You know, Radhika is my good friend. And in the past few days, she has confessed to me that you don't take her calls anymore. Please understand, this is not as simple as you think," she said with a firm voice.

I exhaled heavily.

"Gosh! Shanaya, take a call today. Either you are with me or I am out of your life forever."

"Nikhil, you can't do this to me!"

Furious, I pressed my thumb on the red button on my screen. I kept the phone under the pillow and covered myself with the blanket. It wasn't long before my head vibrated with my phone. Bah! What does she want from me? I disconnected her call and kept it on the side table. I thought to myself – today is not the day when I can understand her point of view.

♋

"Stop buzzing man!" I yelled as the irritating noise of my phone vibrating penetrated my ears.

Irritably, I covered myself completely with the white blanket.

I tried hard to go back to sleep, but couldn't, so I clutched my phone the moment it beeped again. With the corner of my eye, I saw Shanaya's name on it. Hyper, I picked it up.

"Hello," she said.

"What do you want now? Didn't you eat my brain enough last night?" I roared.

"Nikhil, please come downstairs. I want to talk to you once," she requested.

"Don't mess with me, Shanaya. Please disconnect the phone."

My words sounded so rude the moment I heard them. But I wanted her to decide whether she wanted me or not.

"Nikhil, just come out to the balcony. I am standing just outside your door."

Her words drove my sleep away. I frowned. Putting the phone on hold, I threw the blanket off and walked towards the window. "Damn!" I cried. She was actually standing in front of my house.

"What do you want, Shanaya?" I yelled.

"Please come for a minute, pretty please."

"Okay, just wait a minute; I have to brush my teeth."

As soon as I was done, I unbolted the door. My mother stood outside.

"Good morning, beta." Her tone, casual and light. Her face was cheerful as the sky.

"Good morning, mom. I'll be back from downstairs in a minute."

"What happened? Why are you in a rush?" She was intrigued.

"Mom, Shanaya has come."

"What? She is here?" she asked with wide eyes over an exaggerated smirk. "Nikhil, please ask her to come in. I haven't seen her for years now," she complained.

"Mom, please!"

"Okay, sorry, go," she ordered.

I ran off without closing the main door of the house.

♋

As soon as I stepped outside the door, my eyes fell on the face that had turned my world upside down. In her plain red sweater and black denims, she was the prettiest girl in this whole world. Her sullen face made my muscles cringe inwards and I hated myself for speaking rudely on the phone.

I paced towards her. I could feel the icy fear skimming her skin, forcing goose bumps to surface. With my gaze fixed, I put my hand on her flushed cheeks.

Tears rolled from her eyes. "Can I hug you once?" she requested.

Although I was so angry with her, her tears melted me like a snow. I nodded.

"Nikhil, I can do anything for you, but please don't go away from me. I have loved you for a very long time," she claimed as she put her arms around me, caring for nobody. It was the best feeling in the world.

"Let's go somewhere and talk," I whispered.

At Cafe Mocha in Greater Kailash 1, we chose a corner sofa at the end of the cafe, so that no one could interrupt us.

Sitting beside her, I was staring at her face, my gaze intense, all humour was gone, and strange muscles deep in my belly clenched suddenly. She looked away from my scrutiny and stared down at my knotted fingers.

Clandestinely, my eyes gazed at her from beneath my lashes as she looked towards the ceiling. I could watch her all day. Still nervous, she ran her long fingers slowly over her perfectly straight brownish hair. I bit my lip and stared down at my knuckles. I was all graceless and uncoordinated, barely able to get up from my seat without falling flat on my face.

I put myself together and said to myself, 'This is the right time and there is no point waiting.'

I took her hand like one does while proposing and went down on one knee.

Her forehead freckled with knitted brows; she was completely amazed by my gesture.

Gazing profoundly into her smoky eyes, I said, "Shanaya, I love you. You are the one who makes my heart sink in your love. Last few months have been the best time of my life. You know you love me too. I want to leave my life in your hands. Please give me a chance."

Her eyes were glossy. Tongue-tied, she continued staring.

"Only if I could express what is going in my mind," she murmured, looking down at the marble floor.

"Say yes, Shanaya," I said in an expectant voice.

Baffled, she motioned her hands forward and then took them back again.

I smacked my lips hoping she'd get the courage to say yes, this time. I wanted her to understand how serious I was.

Our eyes fixed on each other; a lot of emotions transferred from the bandwidth of our limited vision when she finally leaned towards me, moved my hands to the back of her neck and kept her fluffed lips over mine, followed by her tongue inside of my mouth.

In excitement, I flushed. Perplexed, I chewed her upper lip. She tasted like heaven. I swallowed thickly and tried to make a move, but being jumpy, I failed. It was our first kiss. I felt so light-hearted because I inferred that the answer was yes. The love of my life had agreed to be with me. I thanked my lucky stars for it.

My stomach rumbled as if in hunger. It felt like I was flying in the air. I felt the blood pulse in my veins, a feeling I had never experienced before. My heart pounded like a car engine. My legs lay as if paralyzed; my hands showed no movement either. I let her kiss me for some time and then I returned it with all the passion I could muster.

After kissing for a while, we parted, and she said, "Nikhil, I love you so much and I want to be with you forever," while her hands held mine tenderly.

I hugged her tight. In my mind, I had decided that she was the one for me.

Now that I had the love of my life with me, I was determined to make our love stronger and deeper with time. I hoped that I could walk on this long journey of life holding her hand, smiling and cherishing every moment with her.

Months later, I returned home from my college in the evening, weariness seeping through my bones. I pressed the doorbell of my house when my eyes caught a letter lying on the ground.

Bending down, I took the letter in my hands. Terror overtook my face as it read "From Mahindra Vehicle Pvt Limited".

Six months ago, I had applied for a summer internship in the Mahindra plant in Pune. Since childhood, I had been very passionate about cars. I used to read car magazines, search the Internet for most modern models and novel inventions in this field. I had always dreamt of pursuing master's in automobile engineering from Germany and this internship was a step closer to my dream. I was waiting for it for months now as I wanted to work on the assembly line of automobiles.

Nervous, with my hands shuddering, I opened the letter and started reading.

It read:

Congratulations! You have been selected for our summer internship program.

With my jaw dropped, I threw a punch in the air with all the strength I could muster and yelled, 'Yes, I did it!' I was as happy as a lark.

As my mother opened the door, I almost jumped on her happily.

"What happened, beta?" she enquired with astonishment as she put her arms around me.

"I got selected, Mom. I will be going to Pune for an internship."

"Congratulations, beta! But I don't want you to go away for two months. You are the apple of my eyes." Sadness clouded her features suddenly.

"Mom, it's a part of my dream."

"Okay, I will manage if you are happy. Let's go inside." She faked a smile.

My mother was not in favour of sending me away because she was too attached to me, being the youngest, and from the time when I was very young, I used to always be beside her like a baby monkey clinging to her mother. But I knew she would let me go for this opportunity.

Later, I informed Shanaya about the internship offer letter. As expected, she went ecstatic and congratulated me. She always believed in me, supported and constantly motivated me about my dream.

♋

It was the day before I was about to leave for Pune and I decided to surprise Shanaya. For the past one week, she had been down in the dumps as I'd be leaving.

I had skipped college and drove my car straight to Shanaya's college. Twisting my wrist, I checked the time. It was five minutes to ten. Generally, her first class finished at ten, so I turned on the music system. 'You can love, you can hide, but you can't escape my love,' I heard the melodious voice of my favourite singer Enrique through the speakers.

As I looked outside the window of my car, just like other days, the famous Kamla Nehru College had a crowd in front of it. With an interested eye, I stared at a group of friends that seemed to be playing dumb charades.

After a while, I checked the wristwatch. It said 10.05.

Phew! I can finally call her now.

I took out my phone from my jacket and called Shanaya.

"Hi, can you come outside. I have a surprise for you!"

"Nikhil, are you here or you are just messing with me?" she asked in a loud voice.

"Come fast. I am waiting!" I ordered and disconnected the phone as I adjusted my hair. I wanted to look my best.

It wasn't long before I saw her briskly walking out of her college gate. She turned scarlet when she saw me standing with a bouquet of red carnations, her favourite. Smiling, I saw the glow on her face, which she had every time when she met me. Dejectedly, I sighed, looking down as I would miss this glow during my internship.

My lips widened into a smile as I raised my head. My eyes continued to gaze upon her as she walked towards me. She wore a black dress, plain and simple, which apparently was her USP to look both hot and cute at the same time. Five feet eight inches, she had a perfect body to become a model. The best thing about her was that she was unaware of her prettiness. Her skin was flawless. It was unlikely that she would ever feel the need of putting on expensive products. Her simplicity, her inner beauty and the shine in her brown eyes were the things that had stolen my heart away.

Still lost, I didn't realize that she had come closer until she pulled my cheeks. I frowned and jerked away a little.

"Have you ever missed a chance to pull my cheeks," I complained mischievously, my voice funny and loud.

"Why would I?" Satisfied, she questioned.

"Thank you for this wonderful surprise, Nikhil. I love you!"

"Do you really think I would have left without getting a hug from my darling?"

"Of course not, my pumpkin."

"Let's go to our favourite Café Mocha."

"Yes, please!" she replied.

♋

Thirty minutes later, we reached the café. It was decorated with ancient Greek paintings on its walls and there were lamps on every table, which gave one a pleasant feeling.

A gentle morning breeze swept through the window as we sat on the couch, curling through the flowers kept on the vase on the centre table, and ruffled her curls. I tweaked my nostrils and took a deep breath just to make sure where the fragrance came from, the flowers or her.

She looked so gorgeous that I couldn't help but ogle at her.

Turning my head around to the left, I gave a fleeting look at the DJ and nodded.

Seconds later, she smiled and leaned towards me with ecstasy bouncing all over her face and grabbed me tightly in her arms as she heard the DJ playing her favourite song 'Baby' by Justin Bieber.

A whoosh of air left my mouth as she hugged me.

"Did you ask for the song?" she whispered as she exhaled over my shoulder. Her warm breath sent a shiver down my back. I felt as if my whole body was melting like chocolate in her arms.

"I did, now give me some sugar."

Giggling, she pecked a kiss on my cheek. And then, withdrawing slowly, she looked at the table, amazed that I had already ordered her favourites – Paan Kiwi Hookah and Chilli Paneer. She loved to smoke hookah. Looming closer to the table, she pulled the long pipe towards her mouth, clamping it between her lips. She took an elongated puff of smoke and released smoke in a rhythmic pattern, one ring after the other. The coordination between her lips, throat, and lungs was sheer art. The aroma of paan blended with kiwi was a delight.

"Aahhhh! It had been a long time since I had last smoked," Shanaya said relaxing her shoulders and sagging against the couch.

A while passed and the hookah hadn't released dense smoke. I asked her to let me do it. For a second, I inhaled deeply and then blew the air inward through the pipe, which resulted in the water from the bottom to rise up to the coal. The flavor and the coal got mixed with the water. I became flushed, embarrassed.

"My hookah expert, look at what you did." She laughed so loud after watching this that I saw others looking at us amused.

"I am sorry, things happen sometime. Ha-ha," I cackled as I put a hand over my mouth.

After the lunch, we drove towards her college again.

Later in the car, her eyes were on me, as if she was trying to capture my face in the walls of her heart. I knew she was battling her tears.

With eyes locked on my face, she kept one hand on my cheek. She continued staring, which made me realize the intensity of her love. I wanted to capture this moment deep down in my memory. I couldn't hold myself from hugging her at that moment and took her in my arms. The moment I tightened the grip, her body shook, and her eyes swam with tears.

"I will miss you, Nikhil. Not seeing you every week will be very hard for me. But meet me the day you come back."

Pulling myself away, I took her forehead in my hands and planted a gentle kiss, and then my lips moved towards hers.

"I love you, sweetheart, and I will come back as soon as possible."

I was pretty sure that this distance would not affect our relationship as all I had to do was close my eyes and listen to the whisper of my heart whenever I would miss her.

The day finally dawned. I heaved a sigh as I stood in front of the Delhi Domestic Airport. Standing at Gate No. 4, I felt an emotional turmoil growing inside me.

"Joe, take good care of your sensitive stomach and grasp as much as you can. I will miss you," my mother muttered with her right-hand skimming over my shoulder.

"Oh, come on, mom! I am a big boy now. I will be just fine," I assured her with a long sigh filled with confidence, my eyes fixed on hers.

"But you will always be a little kid to me, beta," she responded with a simper.

"Just give me your blessings, Mom. I know with your hand on my head, I can achieve anything in this world." I bowed down and touched her feet.

As I got up, she leaned forward and kissed me goodbye on my forehead, her expression hardened as she fought back tears.

Turning towards Nikita, my elder sister, I scoffed.

"Yuck! Look at your face, Di. I am not dying, you know. Come on, cheer up!"

Colour had drained out of her face, and her eyelids drooped. We had always been more than just siblings from childhood, best friends rather.

"Love you, bro, and all the very best." My sister moved forward and gave me a tight hug.

Later I crept towards my father while extending my arms for a warm cuddle.

"All the very best, beta, and keep calling." My father wished me with all the warmth he could gather while plastering a smile on his face.

It was already like a typical Hindi cinema going away scene at the Delhi airport and before anybody could notice, I bowed to take their blessings and made to leave towards the entrance, at the side of which was a sign that displayed the details of my flight to Pune.

Tears welled up my eyes as I left all of them, hesitating to take the forward step. I hung there for a while, my left foot hovering in the air, but then, I moved towards the gate, without once looking back.

♋

I could feel the freedom as I walked, the sense of independence that I had never felt before in my life. A few months ago, I would have my hormones tell me I wasn't ready, but now I welcomed the feeling. It was time to come out of my ivory tower. The entire flight I was occupied with blended thoughts of nostalgia and optimism, unable to choose one over the other, missing the past and anticipating the future. I had decided to stay with my cousin, who was also working in Pune.

At eleven, the aircraft touched down. "Boo-yah! Pune it is!" I yelled.

A thin drop of sweat slithered on my face in coherence with the humid weather as I gazed towards the sky while stretching my body at the exit door of the aircraft.

I sprinted towards my booked radio cab to my brother's apartment.

He lived in the outskirts of the city, in the industrial area, as his company was located there. On my way, the vacant roads grabbed my attention, left me comparing notes with the jam-packed Delhi roads.

After an hour-long quest for the right address, I finally reached his apartment. As I searched for the board signs on the road, I saw a blue address plate highlighting the street as 'Pimpri Chinchwad'. Once again, I checked the address on my phone, just to recheck, and found that I had reached the correct address. From my wallet, I handed out the cash to the driver and got out of the cab. While drawing out the luggage from the boot, I saw my brother, Raghav, rambling towards me smiling.

Raghav was a mechanical engineer from Mumbai. With a good athletic build, a little on the darker side and tall, he was noticeably handsome. I remembered that since the teenage days, he had always had a thing for married women.

"Hi brother. Welcome to Pune!" he bellowed, pulling my back towards his chest with his strong muscular hands.

"Hi, bro, how have you been?" I enquired excitedly clasping him towards me.

"It's all good. What about you?" he asked.

"I am doing great. How's your longtime girlfriend Neha?"

"She got married a couple of months to some dick I beat up in college. It's her loss, not mine. Some things are just not meant to be and you have to let it go," he muttered in a tone of despair.

"Damn! I just hope that all the married ladies in this building are safe from your sexual magnetic charm," I joked to digress from the uncomfortable air as we drew away from each other.

"Not the one on the first floor." He gave a dismissive finger with a lopsided grin on his face.

"Fuck! Are you serious dude? Man!! I envy you." I shook my head in disbelief as he laughed.

We climbed up the stairs to his apartment on the second floor. It looked compact. Enthusiastically, I dropped my bags on the floor and traversed through the apartment. It consisted of one room, a small bathroom, and two huge balconies. There wasn't a single piece of furniture in the entire area. Only a mattress lay on the floor.

After freshening up, we went to have lunch in a nearby mess on his Pulsar bike.

At the mess, I noticed fresh vadas being fried in deep oil and diminutive spices. There were also stacks of pav nearby. Vada Pav. I was so fond of it ever since childhood. Both my brother's and my mouths watered.

"Anna! vada pav aur chai!" Raghav requested showing two fingers to the cook in a white vest and lungi as we sat down.

"Is vada pav your favourite?" he asked, smiling, crosses his arms over his chest.

"Yes. When I'm in Maharashtra, it is," I nodded rubbing my palms together.

"Great! So, what are you doing these days?" he asked.

"I am pursuing Mechanical Engineering from Delhi."

"Another mechanical engineer?' he frowned, scratching his nose.

"Yes, and the summer internship is a vital part of the curriculum."

"Thank you, Anna!" he said as a boy probably fourteen years old kept our vadas and tea on the table.

He continued. "Yes, I am sure you will learn a lot from this experience. Will you apply for master's as well after your bachelor's?' he queried with his forehead creased."

"I will pursue Master's in automobile engineering from Germany after completing my graduation," I replied.

"That sounds about right," he motioned his head up and down in approval.

"It's my dream to work in a big automobile company like Mercedes Benz or BMW in Germany, and I think these experiences will shoulder my resume," I replied taking a tentative sip of my tea.

He hummed while tapping his fingers on the table.

"That's a brilliant plan, but I will suggest you learn German as well. As I am working in this industry and if you want your work to be appropriately done, you have to be able to communicate with operators on the assembly or manufacturing line," he implied.

"I've decided that I will learn the language when I return to Delhi. For a visa it's preferred to at least learn the first level, but I am planning to do five levels out of seven," I replied as I took another bite of the vada pav. "These are delicious, man!"

"I know," he replied licking his lips with his tongue and continued. "It's good that you have already planned things. I wish you all the best bro," he asserted as he patted my shoulder.

"Thanks," I said drumming my fingers on the table.

♋

Next morning, my sleep got perturbed with my phone's ringtone 'Californication'. As the lyrics entered my ears, 'Little girls of Sweden, a dream of silver screen quotations', I grabbed my phone. A faint ray of sunlight arrived in the living room from a disoriented hole on the wooden window. I saw Shanaya's name on my phone screen. My lips curled into a smile.

"Good morning pumpkin!" the voice was loud and bright.

"Hi Shanaya! It's morning already?" I asked while arching my back. My chest rose and fell with rapid breaths.

"Yes, Nikhil, get up quickly. You don't want to be late on your first day."

"Ya, will text you as soon as I reach the plant."

"Sure, miss you."

Hurriedly, I got up and ran towards the washroom.

After an hour, I rushed to the plant all brightened up wearing a creased white shirt, my favourite black trousers complementing my blue tie and mundane black formal shoes.

A combination of three buses helped me reach the plant.

I reached the Chakan plant all excited at 8 a.m. sharp. The moment I put my foot forward, the security guard at the entrance gate stopped me.

"Your ID, please?" he demanded while wiping the sweat from his forehead with his fingers.

I immediately took my documents from my bag.

After wearing the spectacles which were hanging loosely on his chest, he carefully scanned my ID proof and internship offer letter.

After a thorough verification, he made a gate pass on his notepad and handed it to me.

I started walking towards the first erosion coloured metal shop. The number of units of the building was countless. On my toes, the farther I tried to see, the more metallic units I saw, which made my body shiver for a brief moment, realizing the fact that I was inside an enormous manufacturing unit of an automobile. I tugged at my shirt collar.

Later, I saw 'HR department' written on the very first building that came my way.

Stepping forward, I pulled the door open and entered. My eyes fell on the receptionist who looked frail, sitting in her big chair, wearing a knee-length skirt and a white formal shirt. Her dark, black hair fell forward over her face. She pushed it backward impatiently, her large tawny-coloured eyes fixed on her computer.

"Excuse me, is the registration for interns done here?" I asked her in a soft voice while adjusting my tie consciously.

She looked up from her computer and like a classic receptionist, she said, "Yes, please be seated!" Her hands pointing towards an L-shaped white leather couch.

Due to the direct sunlight and humid weather conditions outside, I was parched. I licked my lips, trying to wet my mouth. Luckily, a water filter was just beside the receptionist. At the speed of a wink, I got up from the couch and filled one full glass of water. I drank like a person in the desert, who hadn't seen water for months. Gulp! Gulp! Quenching my thirst, I sat back on the couch.

Out of boredom, I clandestinely glanced at the receptionist a few times, and every time, I found her running her hand through her hair repeatedly, and sometimes toying with a lock of hair, which amused me.

After half an hour of waiting, she called out my name and asked me for my documents.

She vigilantly scanned my documents and said, "Here is your ID card. Always keep it with yourself. For the entire internship duration, you are provided with complimentary food and bus service." She extended her hand to pass on the documents.

"Thank you very much, ma'am." Liberated food and bus service at no cost was a delight, I thought.

"Go to the assembly shop of Mahindra Maxximo and contact your mentor there. His name is Manish Kumar."

I nodded and said, "Okay."

The plant consisted of five main shops/ departments: press, welding, body, paint, and assembly. All the shops were interlinked by moving overhead conveyors.

Later in the assembly shop, I was awestruck at the sight of the gigantic machinery, the Q shaped assembly line, overhead conveyors, and more than two hundred operators working together with pin drop silence, operating with all high technology automated machines. I got an impulsive adrenaline rush.

Amazed by the sight, I began my quest for the quality control department again when I found a mid-sized metal-cum glass cabin in the centre of the assembly which read QCD (Quality Control Department) at the top of the entrance door. Although nervous,

I pulled the handle of the glass door and saw two employees, somewhere in their mid-forties, wearing business suits and sitting recklessly on the chairs.

"May I come in, sir?"

"You may," one said hastily.

"Sir, I am looking for Mr Kumar."

"I am Manish Kumar," one of the two executives answered.

I got scared for a moment because he looked seriously precarious. Even with the creased shirt and rumpled hair, everything about him screamed authority and self-confidence – from the tanned skin and strong muscles beneath the rolled-up sleeves, to the way he watched me with those dark, midnight eyes.

I gathered courage and introduced myself, "Good afternoon, sir. My name is Nikhil Gupta. I have come for a summer internship from Delhi."

"Oh, you are the Delhi boy! Please sit. It's very nice to meet you."

"Pleasure is all mine, sir," I said in a daze, placing my hand in his.

"It's very difficult to get an opportunity for an internship in Mahindra," my mentor proclaimed.

"So, tell me about yourself, Nikhil."

"Sir, I am a mechanical engineering student from Delhi. My passion for automobiles has brought me here. I want to learn every process involved in the manufacturing of cars. I belong from a well-reputed business family of metal scrap, but I want to direct my career in automobiles,' I replied.

He was highly impressed by my introduction.

"Very well then. I must inform you that you have to work hard here in order to gain sufficient knowledge. It is six days working and your timings will be 9 a.m. to 6.30 p.m. Your prime task under the quality control department will be to eliminate all the quality concerns occurring on the assembly line of Mahindra Maxximo."

"I am grateful for the opportunity, sir," I replied optimistically.

The introductory interview went great. Now that I was instructed to observe the assembly line from a distance and to pen down each and every small observation I made, it seemed quite exciting as I always wanted to work where cars were made. I was so amazed by the organization's systematic follow-up, and safety rules were honoured by each and every operator very precisely. The assembly line was bifurcated into three parts and each part was handled by a line team leader.

♋

After lunch, I was back on the assembly line trying to grasp every process and automobile component in the car. At 6:30 p.m. sharp I took my notes and walked towards the bus station to reach home, which was moderately far from the plant. When I reached the apartment, I remembered my brother saying that every food stall or a restaurant was three kilometers away, so I decided to make myself a sandwich. I was missing Shanaya so much that I flipped out my phone.

"Hi, just reached home, how are you?"

"I am good and I can't stop missing you, thinking that you are so far away from me is killing me," she confessed gloomily.

"Even I miss you a lot."

"How was your day, Nikhil?" she murmured.

"My day went fine. The interview with my mentor was good. He seemed daunted by my thoughts about and zeal for cars."

"That's very good. How is the plant set-up?"

"It is just amazing, highly automated, and I have been assigned to a quality concern project in Mahindra Maxximo. It is a small multi-utility vehicle well-known in rural areas of India."

"I can infer from your voice how excited you are. Work hard!"

"Yes, of course."

The next morning, at the bus stop, I saw some of the employees of Mahindra waiting. I thanked looking heavenward, "Thank you, god. I didn't miss the bus."

The bus arrived five minutes after I had reached the bus stop. It was similar to a Delhi blue line bus. Quickly, I hopped on the bus getting in line with the other employees and managed to get a seat.

On scrutinizing the others, I observed that every employee in the bus looked like a Maharashtrian. I tried hard to understand the local language, but most of the time failed at it.

It took forty-five minutes for the bus to reach the plant. As I was instructed to note down the habitual quality issues on the Mahindra Maxximo assembly line, I started observing operators working on the line.

With a notepad in my hand, I started making notes of the concerns on each assembly station. In the evening, I had a handful of quality concerns. Approximately at 6 p.m., I walked towards the quality control office to report my work to my mentor. He was sitting in his chair, tired and worn out.

"Good work. You have one week's time to collect all the concerns and then send me a report in Microsoft Excel format. I hope you know how to operate it, and in case of any doubt or question, you can always come to me for guidance," he said very politely, impressed by my work.

"Certainly, sir. I'll make a remarkable report and it will be there on your desk well before time," I said looking into his eyes.

"Great, have a great evening, see you tomorrow."

"Same to you, sir. Goodnight."

My professional career had got a kick-start. I decided to work like the devil for this report, as they say that the 'first impression is the last impression'.

After half an hour, I boarded the bus and while returning to my apartment, I stopped at a vegetable market to buy some stuff for my evening meal – 'the classic sandwich'.

Minutes later, I climbed up the stairs to the apartment. Turning the spare key, I rotated the knob in the clockwise direction and slightly pushed the door open.

'What the fuck!' my subconscious grumbled with my heart almost in my mouth, as my eyes fell on my brother Raghav who was inside of a woman, who I suspected was the married one from the first floor of the building as he had said earlier. I shook my head just to be sure whether it was true or just a figment of my wicked imagination.

Naked and overwhelmed with pleasure, they didn't even notice me, which gave me a brief moment to digest the unexpected scene where both were humping like African gorillas. The woman passionately spanked Raghav as he thrust inside her with her teeth completely sunk in his right shoulder.

"I will fuck you so hard today that you won't be able to walk for days!" Raghav bellowed as his body moved up on her. The harder he pushed, the louder she moaned in pleasure.

"I want more, dammit, give it to me!" she yelled as she pumped a fist and thrust her fist straight over Raghav's face. Bang! The crack of her knuckles on his face muscles echoed through the wall.

"Ouch! Hey, why did you do that?" he frowned and pulled his body away from her.

"Deeper, you pussy," she teased him, biting her lip.

"You will get it hard, bitch!" he replied instantaneously thrusting inside of her again, with his hand now on her throat. She removed her wedding ring from her finger and kept it beside the mattress on the floor.

The woman, probably in the early thirties, had very sharp features. Her dark brown ruffled hair complimented her ice white complexion. Her voice reflected confidence and authority. With the heavy bust, long nipples and thin waist, she kept my eyes glued on to her for a longer period of time than I could have imagined.

"Damn! I miss Shanaya," I mumbled.

Seconds later, my subconscious hit me with self-realization of my illicit behaviour and yelled, 'Shame on you, Nikhil. Get out of here!'

I slowly pulled the door shut without making a sound.

It took another couple of seconds to believe what I had just seen, which gave me a throbbing boner that almost burst my pants.

I sat on the dusty stairs and waited for them to finish. It was one of the most enjoyable as well as embarrassing moments of my life.

Raghav gave me twenty long minutes to wander in the promiscuous zone of my provoked lustful mind and which allowed me to mentally masturbate about it. I heard the faint approaching sound of their footsteps coming towards me and the door knob turned. He came out wearing a T-shirt and boxer shorts.

"Whoa! You scared me! When did you come, bro?" His tone reeked of doubt. I imagined he suspected me of knowing what had just happened inside.

"I just came back from office. I was attending a phone call," I lied through my teeth as I saw the fear vanishing from Raghav's face. He was relieved.

"Hey! What happened to your face? Did someone beat you today? Tell me who it is, I will kill that bastard!" I dramatically blurted, curling my fingers into a sturdy fist.

"Nothing, just a small fight." He gave a dismissive wave of his hand.

"Oh, okay."

"I would like you to meet Mrs Kakkar," he turned his face away from me and nodded his head into the apartment.

I saw Mrs Kakkar approaching towards me in a blue-coloured suit without a dupatta, which highlighted her gigantic breasts.

"Meet my younger brother Nikhil." He cocked his hand towards me.

"Hi, Nikhil,' she said smilingly, completely unaware of what I had just seen."

Standing there quietly was the only option for me. I tried hard to nod and said a silent hello.

"He is really shy," Raghav commented. "Anyway, I hope you got the sugar for your tea." He winked shoving his hands into his pockets.

"You are so generous, Raghav; you gave me a little extra today. I hope it will cover up for at least a week," she claimed, biting her lip seductively.

"I hope that the sugar doesn't last for a week," Raghav responded raising an eyebrow followed by a smirk.

I couldn't stop the wicked smile echoing on my face as I listened.

She glanced at Raghav again, grinned, and started climbing down the stairs. All I could do was to stare at her silently until she finally disappeared from my sight.

"What fresh hell is this? I didn't know that you were actually fucking this beauty," I revealed as I slammed the door behind us.

"What? You know?"

"I heard the moaning, you moron."

"Shit! Anyway, I told you before, but you doubted my abilities," he shrugged with a simper.

I thought for a moment before shaking my head. "I don't understand, she is living alone with her husband and she must be in her mid-thirties and she is already cheating on him."

He shrugged. "So what? Her husband is in a sales job and he is travelling for almost fifteen days in a month. Initially, it started with friendship when I gave her some respite from her monotonous married life. She also has needs and I am just giving her what she deserves. Big deal!"

"It's so simple for you to say that. I don't wanna see you punched in the dick when her husband finds out,' I said as I dodged him with a punch directed towards his face.

"But I am sure you will save me from him," he joked while extending his hand for a high five.

"You are not gonna get it," I retorted, massaging my right temple.

"Anyway, you were supposed to be back by 11 today from your corporate meeting in Bangalore. How was the meeting, brother?" I queried sitting down on the floor.

"The meeting didn't go well, couldn't have been worse, in fact. A complete waste of my time. The client wants the best quality, but won't compromise on the price."

"Story of every client," I retorted.

"It's really frustrating, you know!"

"Don't think much about it. Tomorrow is another day. More opportunities will follow. Brother, if you are familiar with this town, can you show me around, any pubs or cafes, malls or any historical place? I have heard Pune has a magnificent number of inhabitants, especially students," I asked him while digressing from the subject.

"Yes, you are right. We will go out this Sunday."

♋

The next day, while I was missing Shanaya with my chin resting on my fist, gazing outside the window of the company bus, my phone beeped in my hand. It was Shanaya.

"Good morning, how is my life feeling today?"

"Morning indeed, I was just thinking about you."

"Nikhil, I just have one word for you – 'Kanjoos'!" She burst into laughter.

"What?" I asked squaring my shoulders.

"Ha-Ha. You should have called me if you were missing me, you didn't even call me last night."

"Oh, I didn't even know when I fell asleep working on my presentation."

"I almost forgot, all the best."

"Thanks. I hope everything goes fine."

"It will be awesome. Just be yourself!"

"Thanks, bye."

♋

At the plant, my mentor was waiting for me to present my paper. He invited his senior Mr Sharma to the quality control department and the shop leader too.

Unexpectedly, the presentation went really well; it highlighted my communication skills and the way I represented my innovative ideas to improve the quality.

The shop leader said blissfully to my mentor, "He is a catch, make the most of it and I want more work from him as he is new here and can think out of the box. I think it is obvious that he will be going places."

My mentor, with an insinuation of a smile, said, "Most certainly, sir."

In the evening, my mentor congratulated me for the presentation and said, "Nikhil, try to solve more quality issues while keeping in mind the cost of quality solutions. You have seven weeks left here; try to make the most of it."

With great pleasure, I said, "Thank you, sir. I will not disappoint you."

Immediately, I took out the phone from my pocket and texted Shanaya:

The presentation went really well. I think you know me better than I do. :)

The summer internship had almost come to an end and now I was well aware of the meaning of the phrase 'Living on your own and standing on your feet'. During the entire stay, I did the general household chores on my own with a smile: from washing clothes to ironing, cleaning of dishes every day and the apartment twice a week. Apart from that, there were the trips to the supermarket for essentials like common salt, detergent, hair oil, soap, Dettol, etc., which I had never bothered buying when I was at home.

It was the last week and I was meticulously working on my project report. With the help of my mentor, I gathered some of the former intern's project reports in order to have an idea about the format and the content writing. I framed the report in the best possible way as it was very important for my curriculum.

On my second-last day of internship, I completed my report and presented it to my mentor. He was impressed by my work but suggested a few changes. It took me seven hours to finally complete it.

Later in the evening, I was returning to my apartment. As I pushed the door open, I found Raghav all dressed up in a blue round neck t-shirt and hazy black jeans.

"Are you going to a party, bro?"

"Yes, it's your farewell party tonight. Get ready, will leave in ten minutes. My treat!" he announced, putting some gel on his hair.

"Oh really? thanks, man!" I blurted excitedly.

I rushed towards my bag and took out my favourite black t-shirt and denims.

♋

We reached the night club, among the best clubs in town. As I pushed the big brown-coloured entrance door, my eyes widened as I walked into a dusky, dark nightclub. From the distance, I could hear the songs of Coldplay buzzing, providing a backdrop for the clinking of glasses and chattering of hundreds of people. The intermingled smells of smoke and sweat and too many people instantly assaulted my nostrils as I inhaled deeply. The DJ was just in front of the entrance, with a long illuminating bar at the right. Big leather couches surrounded the dance floor in the middle. The crowd looked all energized as they danced away. Most girls were in short one-piece dresses with high heels. The atmosphere was dynamic and the energy around was overwhelming. I kept gazing as my eyes tried to adjust to the imminent tomblike darkness of the surroundings. Bright spots of Heineken beer signs on the wall stood out, illuminating the faces of the crowd, while others disappeared into the contrasting darkness.

With my jaw open, I continued to surf around when Raghav interrupted.

"Come on! Let's have some beer."

"Sure," I nodded.

We staggered through the crowd towards the bar. When we finally reached, I waved at the bartender and ordered a couple of beers.

♋

"I will miss you, Nikhil, especially the sandwiches," he confessed as he seated his butt on the high seat at the bar.

"Ha-Ha! You really made me feel at home, bro and I will really miss the time we spent together."

"I might come to Delhi after a couple of months for office work to attend the Auto Expo at Pragati Maidan. We will definitely catch up," he acknowledged with a smile on his face.

"That goes without saying, bro. And where is Mrs Kakkar, by the way? I am happy that you didn't invite her," I winked, shoving my hands into my pocket.

"Her husband is now suspicious of her having an affair, so he doesn't go out of the town much these days," he revealed and looked away.

"Better be careful, bro," I warned.

"I will be. Anyway, cheers!' he screamed and started rambling towards the dance floor, moving his body in the rhythm to the beat of Akon's song.

"Let's dance, come!"

♋

Next morning, although hung over from the excessive drinking, I reached the plant at sharp 8.30 a.m. It was the last day of my internship. I was so happy and electrified that I was going home, but I was kind of sad that I would no longer be coming to this huge manufacturing plant. On my way, I had bought some famous sweets for my mentor as a token of appreciation for his efforts and guidance.

When I sat on my seat, I saw my mentor walking towards me with his lips wide and his eyes bright.

"Nikhil, I read your report last night. It's very productive and informative. Well done!" He patted my back as I jumped from my seat in courtesy.

"Thank you very much, sir, I am glad! I couldn't have done this without your cooperation and support." I declared.

"Please accept this is as a token of love and gratitude, sir," I said pleadingly as I pulled out the box of sweets from my bag.

"Thank you very much, Nikhil, and I have a surprise for you." He folded his arms across his chest.

My eyes lit up as I heard the word surprise. I couldn't believe my ears. What could it be, I pondered.

He said while smiling, "Seeing your performance, I would like to offer you a job as a quality executive on the assembly line."

Awe transformed my face as his words entered my brain and I was flushed. With my face turned blank, I took another couple of seconds to respond.

"Sir, I am highly honoured," I bowed.

"We could discuss your salary then."

"It will be a great opportunity for my career, but sir, I am sorry to say I would not be able to work here," I replied with a fake smile.

"What? Are you sure? And may I ask why?" His eyes narrowed, his expression tight as his brows knitted.

"I have always dreamed of studying and working in Germany, sir, and as I have planned to study there next year. I have to pass on this opportunity." With an honest heart and a clear mind, I confessed.

"But I must say, Nikhil, this is a once in a lifetime opportunity, you should at least give it a thought. It will escalate your career to a new level."

"I totally agree with you sir, but I am really sorry." I looked down at the floor.

"All the very best then. Don't work today, just relax and don't forget to take the experience letter from the HR department. You can leave early today."

I smiled and he added as an afterthought, "And one more thing. You always call a spade a spade. Don't ever lose that trait."

"Thank you very much, sir. I would like to be in touch."

"Sure thing, have a prosperous future Nikhil." We shook hands.

"Thank you," I bowed again.

At noon, I collected my relieving letter from the HR department and after submitting the indispensable documents, I left early for the apartment as my flight was at six in the evening.

It took me more than a couple of hours to pack my stuff into two big suitcases. I had mixed feelings about leaving. I did spend some happy memories here with Raghav. I kept staring across the apartment, trying to grasp as much as I could in my memory. Also, Pune in the month of June felt like a mini hill station, as rain fell erratically.

I kept my luggage at the gate and kept the spare key under the mat. Once again, I looked inside the apartment. A cloud of emotions passed over me. My body dropped, I shook with sobs, trembled and then turned away closing the door behind me.

♋

At the airport, I scratched my head browsing for my flight number over the information status board. As I scrolled down, my eyes found my flight finally. It was on time. I sighed in relief.

I sprinted towards the check-in counter. Quickly, I darted towards the crew member who greeted me with a forced smile.

"Good evening, sir. May I have your ticket? Please put the luggage on this belt."

I did and handed her my ticket.

She took the ticket and typed my details on her computer.

"Here is your boarding pass, sir. Have a safe flight."

Putting my boarding pass in my shirt pocket, I scurried towards the security check when a poster of flat 30% sale on watches of a top-notch brand caught my attention. Immediately, my sister's beautiful face appeared in my mind. I decided to gift her something special.

Confident that my sister would love the leather strapped chronograph sports watch, I withdrew my debit card from my wallet and handed it to the salesman.

"I will take this one." I pointed towards the watch kept in a glass showcase.

My sister and I had the best relationship one could possibly have between siblings. Before the day I joined my college, we used to share a room since childhood. Although we have one extra room in the house, my father always persuaded us to share a common room until I joined my college. I guess that's why I am so close to her. We share every single thing with each other. Also, she always knew about Shanaya from the first day of our relationship.

Truthfully, I was kind of a follower and had always been influenced by her. Whatever she liked or did, I ended pursuing eventually. Her likes and dislikes were imprinted perfectly over my being.

I boarded the flight on time. It was a two-hour flight to Delhi. I was on my toes, eager to meet my parents. They were coming to pick me. Also, I had planned a surprise brunch with Shanaya the next day. I made a reservation in the restaurant on the twentieth floor of the Le Meridian hotel in Connaught Place.

♋

As soon as the aircraft's door opened at the Delhi airport, I dashed towards the exit gate while quickly grabbing my luggage from the belt. The moment my foot crossed the exit glass door, I felt the bracing, cleansing, and nostalgic air of the city. My mouth had split into a smile.

Cold droplets of monsoon rain fell on my tired face which felt like an energizing drug. With my eyes closed, I took a deep breath. It felt great to be back in in the city.

Gently, sluggishly I opened my eyes and found my parents standing beside a white car. Their faces brightened upon seeing me and their lips widened. When I glanced towards my father – fifty-eight years old, he was in his signature sparkling white shirt, black trousers, and his well-polished black shoes. He was tall, dark and incredibly handsome with an observant stare. His big eyes grew bigger when anticipated with anger which could infuse any human being with fear. His moustache was well trimmed, almost perfectly shaved face, and his hair properly combed. From the early days, he had been conscious of his looks. His appearance spoke volumes about his character. He had been punctual for all of his business meetings, or for that matter, on any other occasion. His neatness and cleanliness reflected discipline and authority.

I grinned, nodding my head, realizing he had not changed even a bit. Why would he? I slapped my forehead.

Suddenly I heard my mother screaming my name and waving her hand. I ran towards her and bent down to touch her feet. She wrapped me in her warm cozy arms.

"I love you, Mom and missed you so much." My eyes welled up as she stroked my back gently.

"Welcome back beta. Surprise!" She moved back and pointed at the white car.

"What?" I flushed. I turned crimson in excitement.

"Thanks a lot, Mom."

My dad walked up to me, "Oh, come on, Nikhil. It's not a big deal, come here, my boy."

I gave him the tightest hug possible.

"Easy, tiger! I can't breathe," he exclaimed as he jerked away.

"Thanks a lot, Dad!"

"Here, take the new car keys." He extended his arm.

Gratitude etched on my face, I took the keys.

As I sat inside my new Skoda, I glanced around sniffing the new car smell.

The car was well equipped with all the modern features and accessories. The drive felt so smooth and comforting.

An hour later, I entered home. I looked around everywhere. Everything looked untouched as the way it was when I had left for Pune. Suddenly I realized how gigantic my home was, especially after staying in a one-room compact apartment and sleeping on the mattress. I was overjoyed to be home.

On the dinner table, I was served my favourite potato dish. My sister returned home in a while.

"Hellooo! My little brother." She pulled my cheeks hard this time, followed by a kiss on my forehead and a tight hug.

"Hi, sis, nice to be back! Let's have dinner."

"Yumm! These potatoes are delicious, Mom."

"Thanks, beta."

"So, Mom and Dad, I got a job offer from my mentor today," I announced and looked at their faces.

"That's awesome! Did you take it?" My father asked as he straightened his back and crossed his legs.

"Wowie! Congrats, Joe!" my sister yelled from the right while squeezing my hand.

"I am not gonna send you away again, Nikhil." My mother reacted as she raised her chin, and rolled her eyes away from me.

"Guys! Will you let me finish?" I asked defensively with my hands in the air, telling them to relax. "I turned it down as I have one year left to finish my graduation and also I didn't want to commit to any job as I might get admission in one of the German universities. My dream awaits me."

"Now that's my boy! Nikhil, I understand you want to pursue your dream and want to go to Germany, but I am not letting you go anywhere else," Mom said with determination.

And then Dad interrupted. "That's entirely your call, son. I believe children these days know what is best for them and also I have seen how passionate you are. We will all be supportive in whatever path you choose in your career." He leaned back in his chair.

"Thanks, Dad. I am blessed to have such supporting parents. I promise I will never let you down."

"I am sure about that, beta," he said as he took another bite of his chapati.

"And, Dad, one very important thing that I would like to confess is that till today you have given me a very promising life. I have seen people struggling every day for bread and butter. I have always gotten everything before I wished for it."

My father's tight expressions turned into a playful smile as he heard me.

"I feel as proud as a peacock at this moment, Nikhil, since you have a sense of realization about life and its necessities now." He paused and then continued. "Just remember these three things that I am going tell you now and you will always gain success in whatever you choose to do."

He showed me the three fingers of his right hand.

"First is, always pray to god; secondly, never underestimate other human beings; and the third, always be compassionate towards other people. Serving them is akin to serving god."

I nodded positively, storing his words in the deepest part of my brain and said, "Dad, I will always keep that in mind. I know with your hand on my head, I will progress in life."

"Joe! I think we've heard enough of your jibber jabber for the day. Let's sleep now." Nikita rose from her seat.

"What?" I screamed.

"Just kidding, bro. Proud of you." She patted my shoulder.

"Wait a minute! I almost forgot..." I said taking out the watch from my pocket.

"This is for you, Di."

Surprised, she took the watch from my hand and quickly wore it.

Her eyes glittered and she snapped me in her arms. "I love it, thanks a lot!"

"You are most welcome! I am going to sleep now, hell tired. Goodnight everyone."

I stood up from the table and walked towards my bedroom as I heard everyone saying goodnight in a chorus.

Back on my own bed after two months, my body felt relaxed. God! That felt so amazing. I took out my phone and dialled Shanaya's number.

"Hey babe, finally I am back!"

"Yayee! My pumpkin returns! First, tell me when we are meeting tomorrow?"

"I will pick you up around 12 from your college. We will go for a fancy lunch."

"That sounds great, where are we going?"

"That's a surprise."

♋

"Wow! I had such a nice sleep!" I yawned satisfactorily on my king size bed, turning and tossing like a crocodile. The room was icy cold, thanks to the air conditioning. I squinted towards the wall clock.

"What the hell! Shit! I am late." It was eleven already. Panicking, I ran towards the washroom throwing away my white blanket as I had to meet Shanaya at twelve.

On my way to her college, my phone vibrated. It was Shanaya. She texted that she had already reached. I was so excited to see her and hug her.

Luckily, in twenty-five minutes, I reached. I glanced around and found Shanaya standing under the shadow of a tree, playing with her cell phone while scratching her nose with the other hand.

She looked gorgeous in a brown knee-length dress. The heavenly sight made my heart skip a beat.

Her face glowed like the sun as her eyes fell upon me. I parked my car in the service lane and got out. I ran almost jumping on my feet. She briskly walked towards me with a magnificent smile on her face.

Rushing towards her, I clutched my hands around her. The feeling was sensational as if the clock stopped ticking, birds stopped chirping and sun stopped shining; the world around us was stagnant for the moment, hoping to resume after this short trip to heaven. I sniffed over her shoulder. Her fragrance gave a knock on my head and tingled my senses. It felt as if our bodies were getting charged up by our body heat. My hands went on from her back to her face and we parted. Our eyes locked on to each other. I could feel her hand over my chest. I kept on looking into her eyes, wanting to show her how much I had missed her these two months. She bit her lower lip and her chest rose and fell with rapid breaths. My lips met hers and we kissed. They say, the perfect kiss is the one which comes after staring into each other's eyes and letting the body move by itself without taking help from the brain cells. I could feel the warmth on her lips and love in her breath. Her body reacted as if it knew that I had come back. For the next two minutes, we were kissing each other passionately, not worrying about the people around.

"God knows how much I have missed you in these two months, babe. Love you to the moon and back."

"I love you more," she replied while blushing.

"Shall we?" I said, insinuating with my hand to walk towards the car.

"Whose car is this?" she asked with her eyebrows raised.

"Surprise! Dad gifted it to me," I said excitedly.

"What?" she flushed.

"Yes, ma'am, will you do the honours and sit inside?"

"Congrats Gupta ji! Your parents pamper you so much."

"Yeah."

"If you go to Germany for two years, they will buy you a private jet when you come back."

"Be that as it may, it will be awesome Shanaya. We will fly around the world together." I giggled.

"Ma'am, please be seated," I requested opening the door for her.

"Now tell me, where are we going?" she asked as she pulled herself inside the car.

"That's a surprise!"

♋

In twenty minutes, we reached Le Meridian on Ashoka Road near India Gate.

The restaurant was on the twentieth floor of the hotel.

At the elevators, I pressed the call button, and the bell rang after a while. The doors slid open, revealing a young couple cuddling. Embarrassed, they jumped out, staring guiltily in every direction, but ours. Shanaya and I stepped into the elevator. As soon we entered the vacant elevator, I pushed her into the corner. She frowned. I don't know what happened to me all of a sudden. But there was an adrenaline rush. I wanted to kiss her. I raked my fingers through her hair. My lower body was touching hers. Our heartbeats accelerated. She kept her hand around my neck. I couldn't wait any longer. With a jerk, she pulled me closer, and I put my lips on hers. My hands massaged her back as I opened the zipper; the soft touch of her skin was exquisite, and it was as soft as velvet.

"Mmmm!" She chewed on her lip, her eyes burning with pleasure.

My lips travelled to her right ear with my tongue gently licking her skin. My one hand grabbed her butt and the other one cupped her breast.

"Shhh!" She shivered taking a sharp breath.

I let my hand make the move again for a while and she put her arms on my back, now trying to dig inside the bottom layer of my skin. Her lower lip shuddered. We stood tantalizingly close for the first time in our relationship.

All of a sudden, she pushed me away and whirled around, and her back was in front of my face.

"You are so beautiful Shanaya!" I whispered with my warm breath gliding on her shoulder.

I brushed her hair from her neck to the front and leaned in, sniffing her shoulder while my tongue swirled over it.

Before I could control myself, my teeth dug into her shoulder.

"Ouch! God!" She trembled with desire.

Her hand brushed my thigh. A shudder ran through my skin, goose bumps erupted. My blood flamed and moved towards the south of my body giving me a boner, and I flushed. We were so close to each other that even air couldn't pass through. She bounced on her toes as I slid my hands from her pelvis to her thigh.

We had lost track of the elevator movement. The bell rang and the door opened on the twentieth floor. Freaked, we parted quickly. I adjusted my t-shirt while she zipped up her dress.

It was for the first time that we got so close. Although we were pleased, there was an absolute silence for a minute as we tried to catch our breath.

We walked towards the restaurant holding hands. Shanaya threw a naughty look as she brushed her shoulder with her fingers. I grinned.

"I wish the elevator hadn't opened for another ten minutes," I said with a smirk.

"You would have eaten up my shoulder, you freak!" She blushed, her cheeks turning pink.

"Have you not heard of love bites before?" I asked teasingly while pressing her hand hard.

"I have, but you would have pierced my flesh, I am sure." She winked at me.

The manager on the outside desk jumped up from his seat as he saw us approaching towards him.

"Good afternoon, sir, madam. Do you have a booking?"

"Yes, it's in the name of Mrs and Mr Gupta," I replied.

Shanaya looked at me with her raised brow and then her mouth turned into a smile. She was speechless by the gesture.

"Yes, sir. Please come!"

The manager guided us to a table near a very large window. We sat on the chairs across each other.

The moment we looked outside, awe transformed on our faces. The Chinese restaurant was the capital's highest rooftop indeed. The panoramic view of the city took all our focus. We almost stretched up from our seat for more. Clouds felt nearer, birds, especially eagles were flying in large numbers.

"Can you believe it? Almost every part of the city is visible from here!" I exclaimed with my eyes fixed on the outside view.

"It's astonishingly beautiful. Look, that's India Gate on the right." She pointed out with her long index finger.

"Yes, and look the Rashtrapati Bhavan on the left and that's Qutub Minar on the far right," I said.

"Thanks for bringing me here, Nikhil. How did you know about this place?" she asked as she leaned back in her chair.

"I have come here with my ex…" I said, with my arms on the table with my palm supporting my chin.

"What? But you never told me that you had a girlfriend. Did you come here with Radhika?" Her eyes scorched with anger.

"I mean, uhh…"

"You better speak up quickly or you will get a punch on your face." Her hands squeezed into fists.

"Not on the face, please!" I blurted dramatically, putting my hands in front of my face.

She was breathing hard. Her gaze was fixed, and all the humour gone. She kept tapping her finger on the table.

"You better come up with a good explanation," she said looking at me intently.

"No, stupid. I am just fooling around with you. Come on, you know I never had a girlfriend before. But I must say, I really liked seeing the jealousy rise in you," I grinned rubbing my chin.

She let out a harsh breath, rolled her eyes from me and leaned back in her chair.

"Uff! Let's order now. I am famished. I am tired of your shenanigans," she said grabbing the menu from the table.

The menu was exquisitely intended with the impeccable flavour of luxury and we ordered quickly.

After half an hour, the food was served. The Manchurian especially was delicious and the noodles were prepared with healthy boiled vegetables. After finishing lunch, we went for a short drive to India Gate. The weather was a little breezy and for the month of July, it was slightly cold. Eventually, I dropped her near her home and went back to mine.

♋

My college began the next week. I was then in the seventh semester of mechanical engineering. When I reached college, I felt so different that suddenly, from a professional of an automobile manufacturing plant, I was again a student. I had to attend classes regularly, work on assignments, presentations, lab work, viva and what not.

I learned that this semester we had some management subjects like ERP (Enterprise Resource Planning), Supply Chain Management and Risk and Value Management along with the core engineering subjects. Being from a business family, I was always inclined towards business; I thought it would be very exhilarating.

Later in the class, every other mate was sharing their industry experiences with their friends. The class environment was way more encouraging and upbeat than before. Apparently, the industry exposure had groomed everyone to behave like a professional engineer.

My first class was Mechatronics. I could not concentrate much as I used to, maybe because I had been a little out of touch with college life. Moreover, our faculty dropped a bombshell when he announced that we had to submit our internship project report after a couple of weeks and an external viva next month.

Also, along with college studies, I had started preparing for GRE (Graduate Record Exam) which was the entrance exam for German universities. Getting admission into a German university was not a piece of cake. One should have a complete package: good academic score, at least 320/340 in GRE, work experience, project works, internships, statement of purpose letters, recommendations from college professors and on top of all, basic knowledge of the German language. Also, due to almost no tuition fees, the competition was extremely tough, and every semester only three to four Indian students were admitted per college. But I decided to chance my arm anyway.

As planned, I had registered myself for German classes in Max Mueller Bhavan Goethe Institute on Kasturba Gandhi Marg Delhi.

"Hurry up Nikhil, you don't have much time," I said panicking and stealing a glance at my wrist watch. Damn! Just one minute left. I threw my hand in the air, in an attempt of relief from rigorous writing I had been doing for the past three hours, but I still had to carve in few lines for my last answer.

"Bzzzzzzzzzz!" I heard the loud and clear, yet annoying sound of the exam bell. I put a full stop to my answer and put a cap on my pen.

"Phew," I sighed with relief.

God! Finally, my last semester exams were over. I was a mechanical engineer now; it was an overwhelming, joyful sentiment. My fingers turned into a fist and I threw it in the air throwing a silent 'Yes I did it!' I leaned back on my desk, arching my back. There was a cacophony of clapping and high-fives in the examination hall.

Spinning my head around, I took a quick peek at my classmates, who were in high spirits, hugging and applauding each other. And then I saw my classmate Jai coming towards me.

"Congrats, bro!" He yelled as he inched forward for a full sided hug.

"Same to you, finally we are engineers," I replied hugging him, clutching my hands around his back.

"What's next, Germany? How was your score in GRE?" he asked as we drew apart.

"I scored 322. Fingers crossed. Application results could be out anytime soon. It's been four months now since I have been kept on tenterhooks."

"Awesome score man! Proud of you." He patted my shoulder.

"What have you planned for yourself? Job placement?"

"Yup! Got selected in Maruti Suzuki." He nodded with pride.

"Great man! Congrats," I wished him with a thumb up.

"Thanks! All right, will meet soon, bye." We shook hands before parting.

My exams had gone exceptionally well this time. I had really worked hard this semester and tried to give my best. It was now just results of the application to the German universities that I had to wait for, and if I got lucky, I would be studying in Germany this year.

Rambling towards the parking lot, with Germany sweeping all over my mind, I wanted to celebrate. Maybe I would steal that expensive whiskey stacked in my dad's almirah, I pondered with a mischievous smile.

My body shivered with exhilaration while I daydreamed about living in a foreign country and working in magnificent automobile companies like BMW and Mercedes-Benz as I drove home. I was contented as everything was going according to plan in my life. Life seemed perfect at that moment.

♋

Almost after an hour, I reached home. My lungs inflated as I took a deep breath and got out of my car. Hurriedly, I climbed up to the first floor and pressed the doorbell.

Ding-Dong

I rocked back and forth on my heels. My eyes waited for my mother to open the door. I rubbed my palms together. Nobody answered.

Impatiently, I pressed the bell again.

Dinggg-Doonngg

I heard the stretched sound of the doorbell, as I pressed the bell for a longer time.

Two minutes had passed and no one came out. I sagged against the wall and loosened my shirt button wondering why no one had answered the door yet. Dad may have left for work, but my mother was usually home. And even if she was away, she always sent me a text, I thought.

Finally, I entered the lock key on the phone screen which was 1965, my mother's year of birth, and dialled my dad's number.

After a couple of rings, he picked up.

"Dad, I am standing outside, where are you and mom?" I asked massaging my chin.

"Son, we have come to a hospital for a checkup."

As soon as my ears heard the word hospital, my body jerked.

"Hospital? What happened, Dad?" I frowned.

"Nothing to worry, your mom has some sort of cyst in her breast which she showed me this morning, so I thought we should go and get it checked. Your sister is with me."

"Cyst?" I asked slacked-mouthed. "Since when did she have this?" I asked again desperately to know more.

"She says since the past couple of months," he revealed.

"Okay. I am coming to the hospital right now."

"Drive slowly, beta!"

I sat down on the stairs. My knees were shaky. "Damn! God! What is this?" I shrieked looking heavenwards, my hands resting on my cheeks. "God please don't let anything happen to my mother," I said to myself.

I got up quickly and sprinted towards my car. A wave of ugly thoughts hit my head and it made my flesh crawl! I shook my head and prayed to god.

I couldn't start the car. Nervously I looked around and saw Shanaya's name on my phone's screen.

"Shanaya!" I cried disregarding the lump in my throat.

"Hi. How was your exam?"

"Shanaya, my parents are in the hospital right now and I am going there." My breathing quickened.

"What? Nikhil, what happened?" she queried, her voice brimming with concern.

"My mother has a lu... lump on her breast," I stammered as the muscles in my stomach had twisted.

She exclaimed, "What?"

"My father said that she has a cyst in her breast and it's been there for the past couple of months. She told my father about it today and they've gone for a checkup," I told her, curling into a ball.

"It's okay Nikhil; let's not get worried unless we have to." Her voice oozed confidence.

"Really?" I asked with wide eyes.

"Yes, you don't have to worry about it; it could be just a normal collection of mass and nothing else," she said convincingly.

"Okay, I am going there now. Will keep you posted," I said sensing her trepidation. She was holding herself together. Her words boosted positivity in my head. I straightened my back and put my arms on the wheels and switched on the ignition.

"Nikhil, just have faith in god and your mother will be absolutely fine, trust me."

"Thank you very much for saying that. Bye."

♋

At the hospital, I saw my mother from the distance, sitting in between Dad and Nikita. My knees felt weak, my heart almost in my mouth as I saw her gloomy face with her eyebrows raised, and drawn together, muscles in her face tight.

Stirring away the pessimism, I scurried towards her. It was the time to be brave.

Her eyes fell on my face as I approached her. She smiled.

"Mom, I love you so much." I pecked a kiss on her cheek as I bent forward and then hugged her tightly.

She hugged me back. Her body trembled with terror. Tears rolled down her eyes.

"Mom, you will be absolutely fine, and don't worry, test results would be negative," I convinced her while rubbing her back.

"Yes, of course, Nikhil. The doctor has already taken the cyst sample for biopsy. Mark my words, we will be home in an hour. There is nothing to worry," Dad Interrupted as he kept his hand over my shoulder. His touch added strength to my sinking confidence. My sister's and mother's faces also brightened up as they heard him.

"Mom, you didn't ask me about my exam?" I asked digressing from the elephant in the room.

"Oh yes, I almost forgot. Tell me, how did it go?" she asked raising her head up, her eyes wide.

"The exam was good. Finally, your son is a mechanical engineer. Today seems to be a good day, so nothing can go wrong," I said out my thoughts aloud.

"Congrats, beta. I am proud of you!" she said putting her hand on my head.

"But I am really worried about the test results," she added as she turned her hand into a fist and kept it on her lips.

"Mom, everything will be fine. After all, you did not have any kind of symptom or pain or any kind of uneasiness before."

"Joe, I am so worried," my sister whispered inching closer.

"Sis, just relax. Everything is gonna be just fine. I believe in god and his theory of karma. Our mother has never done anything wrong in her entire life. She has been benevolent and compassionate towards every human being. She will be fine."

♋

We waited for another two hours when suddenly I saw a nurse walking towards us.

"Please come inside the cabin. The doctor has called you all."

I bit my tongue in fear and once again prayed to god, folding my hands as I shut my eyes tightly.

In unison, we all got up and walked into the cabin.

It was a compact and neat room with a wooden table in front, a large single patient bed behind the doctor's chair, semi-covered with a white curtain. A large colourful poster of a woman's breast with proper labelling of each of its part was framed on the left wall. My body shook as my eyes fell on the big posters of breast cancer on the right wall.

The lady doctor sat on her big comfortable black chair. She was probably in her mid-forties, wearing round spectacles, blinking owlishly as she read the reports. She looked up.

"Well, let me come to the point. She has been diagnosed with breast cancer, but you don't have to worry as it is easily curable these days. It is in the first stage," she declared.

I gripped the arm of the chair; my body went numb, drowning in the sea of grief as I heard her. My eyes welled up.

Scared, I turned my face towards mom and found her looking terrified. The grief surged on her every breath. Her forehead wrinkled. She was fighting back tears as her eyelids blinked rapidly. Suddenly, she clasped me in her arms and tears began to spill on the bare skin of my shoulder. A shudder ran down my bones. For me, it was the worst feeling in the world.

My soul shrieked in vain. 'Why god? Why has this happened to my angelic mother? Why do you always give illness to nice people on earth? Only today I was daydreaming and was so happy, and now you've taken that happincss away from me.

People often say don't smoke, you might suffer from lung cancer. Don't drink alcohol or you will be rewarded with a corroded liver. My mother never drank, smoked or did anything bad of that sort, but still, god planned this for her. Fate and destiny played well with my life today, I meditated.

Mom had always taught me to respect and be satisfied with whatever god has blessed us with. Until this day, I always had complete faith in god, but this time, my faith was shaken. I could not think straight anymore.

Sauntering further in my agonizing thoughts, I realized that until this morning she had been a healthy human being doing her daily chores, and within a few hours she was diagnosed with breast cancer. Rerunning the moment I shared with her in my head this morning, when I touched her feet before going for the exam, who would have thought we'd be in this situation a few hours later.

It would have been the best thing in the world if this would have been just a dream and everything would come back to normal when I got up. But, this is life – things will never turn out the way you want them to.

♋

It was the dawn of the day of mom's breast removal surgery. My life had changed so much in a week. The entire week we hopped from one hospital to the other, taking second opinions.

Finally, we decided to go for the surgery from the first doctor who had diagnosed the cancer. She was the most experienced oncologist in India. We felt confident.

On the way to the operation theatre, my mother gripped my hand tightly as she lay on the stretcher.

"Son, take care of your father, he appears as hard as stone, but he is very emotional right now." She blanched as a line appeared between her brows.

"Oh, come on, Mom. You are just coming back in an hour. And yes, I will take care of him," I replied cheerfully. Only god knew how scared I was.

She forced a smile after she heard me and probably anaesthesia took charge as she closed her eyes. The nurse closed the operation theatre's door and I saw the red light come on atop the door.

Dad, Nikita and I sat down on the bench just outside the operation theatre. Dad went blank. He stretched his legs and crossed his arms over his chest. With his eyes closed, he took a few deep breaths.

Nikita rested her head on my shoulder. With a scowl on her face, she constantly rubbed her hands on her thighs. Her mouth set in a hard line.

I was numb and constantly praying to god for this operation to be successful and for mom to be healthy again and free from such an ugly, life-threatening disease. Suddenly I felt a vibration in my pocket. Ignoring it completely, I held my sister's hand. It felt good. In reflex, she lifted her head looking at me and passed a smile, keeping her head again on my shoulder. My phone beeped again. Without moving my body, I pulled out the phone and saw an email notification. The email address highlighted on the screen looked familiar. It was from one of the German universities I had applied to. Perplexed, I kept my phone on the side. I waited, tapping my fingers on my lap and was unable to sit still. I couldn't stop myself from thinking about the email.

And then bowing down in the face of my curiosity, on the screen pad, I typed the unlock code and clicked on the email.

Holy shit!! My pupils flared as I read 'Congratulations' on the screen.

It was an admission letter from the University of Munich. For the moment, my heart was divided with anxiety for my mother, and excitement for my achievement. Finally, my dream was a reality now. I bit my nails.

I cocked my head left, scratching my beard and rolled my eyes to the right, wondering what god was up to. A wide smile involuntarily appeared.

My sister sat straight and saw my lopsided grin.

"What happened Joe? Why are you smiling?" She asked bug-eyed.

"I feel as if fate is mocking me right now." I smacked my forehead and shook my head in disappointment.

"What?" she muttered with her expressions tight and gaze unnerving.

'I've got admission into one of the German universities," I retorted. My mouth snapped shut as I looked away from her.

She didn't know how to react, so she kept quiet and waited for me to speak.

"Oh god! Can there be a more cruel mockery of fate?" I said out loud looking upwards.

"Why would you say something like that?" she queried, skimming my forearm with her hands sympathetically.

"The dream means nothing to me now. I can't go to Germany," I confessed shaking my head. "I will stay forever with mom now," I decided, knowing that I was crossing the Rubicon.

"Joe, just relax, when mom will get healthy, we will send you there." She held my shoulder tightly.

"No Di, I don't want to go now." I shook my head again. "I can't miss even a single second with mom."

"I guess you are right." She nodded, sadly curling her lips together.

God had played really well with my life in the span of a week! It seemed everything is already written or rather planned to happen in life. What's the point of doing anything in life? It seems as if when the time comes, life will just tap you on your shoulders and say, 'Hey, buddy, cancel all your plans and forget about your dreams, isn't gonna happen because I have planned something else for you.' I pondered cursing the cruelty of life.

Suddenly my sight fell on the red operation theatre light as it turned off. Within seconds, the door opened and the doctor came out.

We soared from the bench in an instance.

"The operation was successful; she will be shifted to the room in a couple of hours," she informed removing her gloves.

Her words calmed my soul and I let out a soothing and a relaxing breath.

"Come here, you two," my father requested signalling from his hands.

Nikita and I put our arms together.

I felt so relieved and thanked god.

"God! You take away anything you want from me in my life, but just keep my family healthy and together," I murmured.

♋

In the evening, mom was finally shifted to the hospital room. She was half-conscious as the anaesthesia still had its effect on her. She lay straight on the patient's bed.

"Mom," I murmured.

She glanced at me, a smile slipped onto her face.

"Did you have your lunch?" she queried.

"Yes, Mom, I did. I knew you would ask, so as soon as we were told that the operation was successful, we all ate together," I replied stroking her hair.

"Okay. Please take good care of yourself, Nikhil."

"Of course Mom, I will. Don't worry and get some rest."

I was taken aback. She had just came out of this big surgery and the first thought that came to her mind was whether her children had had lunch or not. For me, my mother is greater than god. In life, god gives you a lot of things and then takes it all away, maybe to teach us a lesson; on the other hand, my mother always showered love and happiness on me without expecting any appreciation or anything in return. She never took anything away from me.

Next morning, I was sitting comfortably on the black sofa in the hospital room with Mom and Dad. My mind was constantly debating whether to tell them about the admission or not. But a few minutes later, I thought it was time to tell them that I would not be going to Germany.

"Mom and Dad, I got the admission in Germany," I announced smiling.

My mother looked towards my father and smiled.

"Congratulations, son! When is your semester starting?" My father gazed at me.

"Dad, I have decided that I will join our family business and not go to Germany. I want to spend the entire life with my family."

"Nikhil, but it was your dream," Mom interrupted, completely amazed with her eyebrows knitted together and eyelids blinking like a butterfly wing.

"Mom, I saw a new dream today. A dream in which we all live happily ever after and I want to cherish every single second with you."

She went blank, her moist eyes fixed on mine.

"I love you, Nikhil. I am so relieved today; I can't tell you how worried I was about you going to another country."

"From now on, I will try my best to be a good son," I added sitting straight on the couch.

"But you are already a very good son." My father got up from his chair and clutched me in his arms.

"Dad, from next Monday, I will be working with you," I replied hugging him back.

"Sure, son. I have been dreaming my whole life that one day my son will take over," he said with a big smile on his face while patting my back.

"I will not disappoint you, you have my word," I added.

♋

Monday morning, I was preparing a club sandwich for myself in the kitchen. Since last year, when I returned from Pune, bread had been my favourite pick for a light breakfast.

I picked up the salt and pepper shakers from the top shelf over the big L-shaped counter and sprinkled them one by one on my half-done sandwich. I suddenly heard Dad's voice from the living room louder than the growling sound of my stomach.

"Nikhil, get ready. We are getting late for office."

"Yes Dad, in a minute," I replied, quickly wiping the mess on the counter.

It was my first day at work. I had woken up on time by Shanaya's call in the morning. I wondered if I could ever get up or be on time anywhere without her.

Apathetic and demotivated, having to digress from my childhood dream of Germany and settling for the family business, I pulled myself together and came out from the kitchen with a fake smile. I had lost the battle this time; after all, who can win against fate.

"Good morning, Nikhil," my mom greeted as she got up from the bed. Her face was swollen since the past couple of days and she had been weaker as it took more time than expected for her to recover from the surgery.

"Morning."

"Nikhil, all the best for your first day, you will love this work eventually as you will be able to travel the world during international conferences."

"Mom, that is the only thing that excites me, but it is just a couple of times a year. What about the rest of the days?" I shrugged, eyebrows raised.

"Don't be cynical about it, give it a try."

"Hmm. I will," I murmured.

After finishing my breakfast, I rushed towards the car.

Our workplace was located on the outskirts of Delhi in the Industrial Area – an hour's drive from my house.

I had a very bizarre feeling as I sat beside Dad in the backseat of the car. In early days, I had thought about how would it feel to go to the office with Dad, but never thought it would feel this strange.

Throughout the drive, my father briefed me about the business. He started with the procurement of metal scraps from the western countries, and then the process of segregation, followed by sales.

The driver pushed the brakes in front of the gigantic black iron gate of the segregating plant and pressed the horn.

As the car entered, my eyes widened the moment I saw almost a hundred women working over the scrap metal.

"Dad, how come we have women working for us?" I asked with curiosity.

"Nikhil, these women are extremely skilled and trained. They can hand-segregate any type of metal very quickly and they live in a nearby village."

"It's very astonishing, Dad."

"We have men as well, but they generally load and unload the material and work in the formation of metal cubes using the pressing machines. Let's go."

I stormed out of the car on the sand floor. Loud noises of machines vibrated in my ears. Also, dust particles tweaked my face and I could see them accumulating on my white shirt. The scorching heat and the direct exposure of the sunlight burning my skin spurred my agitation. I fanned my heated face with my hands.

"Get used to it Nikhil. Come, I will show you the office," he said walking towards his office.

I stood there on my spot, vexed.

'Stop complaining dude, calm down! There's no need to get all steamed up about it. Your father has been doing this for years, and you can do this too.' My subconscious tried to convince me.

Finally, I walked towards the office located on the left side of the entrance gate. My father sat in his big black chair concentrating on a few documents quietly. I looked around the room. A small compact, square room with a marble floor, white walls, a table and three chairs. The table was a mess with lots of papers and files scattered all over it. And the wall behind his chair had a gigantic picture of Shiva. I bowed down my head folding my hands with a silent prayer and walked outside the office to observe the process.

♋

It took me almost four hours to monitor and learn about all the processes meticulously. From large bailing/pressing machines to belt conveyors, metal purifies and hand sorting of the metals, I tried my best to grasp everything.

Seconds later, while wiping the sweat from my forehead, I strolled towards the office.

"Let's go home, Nikhil," my father ordered as he packed his stuff into his black leather bag.

"So Nikhil, ask me any questions related to the process," he asked in the car.

"Not at the moment. I will go through it tomorrow once again and will let you know," I replied.

"Once you gain ample knowledge of the material and the process, I will introduce you to the buying process," he added as he scrolled down his mailbox on his phone.

"Dad, I guess I will be good at it. And since I have a firm knowledge of French and German, I think communication will be very effective.'

"I knew it, that's why I have always asked you to learn new languages. Remember one thing in life, you can lose your money, fame and wealth with time, but knowledge is something which can never be taken away from you. It is your actual wealth earned indeed." He pointed his index finger at me.

"That's very well said, Dad. It's so true."

"Sure, son, continue your classes. Join the weekend batch. You can work with me on weekdays."

After almost an hour, I reached home.

"Here comes the businessman," Nikita cackled as I stepped inside the house.

"Ha-ha. Good one, sis," I simpered.

"Freshen up, let's have dinner," she requested as she walked towards the kitchen.

I took off my shoes and scurried towards my mother's room while opening the top button of my shirt.

Mom was watching her favourite daily soap in her room, resting comfortably on her king size bed. The moment she saw me coming, she picked up the remote and lowered down the television volume.

"Good evening, Mom," I said sitting beside her on her bed with my hands resting on my lap.

"Oh. You are back," she retorted. Her face appeared pale and she had lost quite a bit of her hair because of the chemotherapy.

"Yes, Mom. First tell me how are you feeling? Any side effects of chemotherapy?"

"I am feeling better, Nikhil, and no major side effects," she said and quickly added, "So how was your first day at the office? My son is now going for work. It is a proud moment for me."

"Mom, it was good. I learned a few things. Even though it's not that interesting, but I think I will be able to fit in," I lied through my teeth as I was thinking completely the opposite of what I had said.

"That's great. I am sure about that and remember one thing – pleasure in the job puts perfection in the work." She ran her fingers through her hair.

"I hope so," I said nodding, trying to understand her point.

♋

A couple of months later, it was already three in the afternoon and Shanaya had been waiting for me for the last thirty minutes. God! I hope she wasn't angry this time as I always got late due to one reason or the other. I finally parked my car on the outer circle of Connaught Place, and cruised towards the restaurant. I impatiently looked around for her when my eyes finally found her sitting patiently on the black couch, resting her chin on her palm with her arms crossed over the table. Her face brightened up as she saw me coming. She looked extraordinarily gorgeous in her red Ed-Hardy t-shirt and blue denims.

How can anyone look so astonishingly smoking hot in such simple clothes? I ruminated. Maybe that's her thing, simplicity at its best, or maybe my eyes did some magic trick in my head which made me feel that she was the world's most beautiful girl alive.

"You look so beautiful today, Shanaya. I have missed you so much," I confessed.

"Thank you, I can't tell you how difficult it was to not meet you at this point in your life," she murmured as she pulled me into her arms.

"Mmm! It feels great melting in your arms, like a chocolate. I was hoping that this day would get better and it did," I said as my muscles loosened and I took a deep breath.

"Can I eat this caramel filled chocolate? Dairy Milk or Mars?" She laughed, seductively rolling her eyes.

"Sure. I am all yours."

We sat down on the couch.

It had been over a month since I last met her and I couldn't stop myself from staring at her.

"Why are you looking at me like that? I feel shy."

"I am just admiring your beautiful eyes. Can I say something?"

"Yes, please,'" she replied raising her chin.

Looming closer, I pushed her hair back from her face.

"Your beauteous brown eyes, hazy and bright at the same time, take me to the world unravelled, which flaunts the sunshine in the moonlight. And the best part is that I could never tell if it's a dream or a lie," I whispered looking straight into her eyes.

Fascinated, she bit her lip and glanced down at her soft hands, and then up again at my face. Instantly, she put her arms around my neck while looking in my eyes, came closer and glided her soft lips into mine. Her strawberry flavoured lip balm added flavour to her delectable lips. Consequently, my hands went skimming her back. 'God! I want to kiss her forever,' I thought.

But after a while, we parted, remembering we were in a restaurant.

Embarrassed, we looked towards the people around and burst out into laughter.

"How was the chemotherapy? Is your mom fine?" she asked digressing from the wave of sensual thoughts.

"It was okay. We all went to the hospital together. She was fine until we reached there."

"Then what happened?"

"As soon as nurse injected the dip in her right hand, she started crying."

"But why? Was she scared?"

"She was indeed. I tried to convince her that she would be fine in a few months and the therapy is not at all painful. I lied about the treatment to her."

Shanaya listened quietly and held my hands.

I went on. "Then Nikita and I held her together. Mom said that because of her, we had to go through so much. She was the one who was suffering every day, but still she was thinking about us."

"Oh really," she said.

"How can anyone be so selfless? I guess mothers are like that only; for them, children come first every time."

"Nikhil, your mother is so sweet. She has always been like that."

"Shanaya, it's not easy to watch your mother cry in your arms."

"I can empathize," she said while kissing me on my right cheek as she massaged my neck.

"I don't know, it's been a while now, I don't feel good about life. I have joined my family business; my mother is not well. My life is so not what I had imagined. Once a week I go for chemotherapy with Mom, German classes on weekends and weekdays in office. I don't know, but I feel everything has changed now and there's nothing to look forward to these days." I rolled my eyes upwards, dejectedly.

"Shhh! Look at me." She put her index finger on my lips.

"Nikhil, I am telling you it is just a phase, you will get over this and mom will be healthy again. Everything will be fine. Nothing is permanent here. When a tree can endure the cold callous winter season which leaves it desiccated and pale, and can wait for the spring to rejuvenate it again, then we being humans can be patient and wait for the good times; it is always good after the bad.

"Every day is followed by a night. The night just before the morning is known to be the toughest one. Similarly, this is the toughest phase of your life. Once you pass this, a new bright morning will welcome you."

I was amazed by her comparison and was motivated.

"Shanaya, you are such an optimistic person and I love that about you. Always encouraging me when I feel low. I don't know what would I have done without you. I was torn a few minutes back, but I feel much better now."

"Don't say that. I am always with you, no matter what, for life and beyond."

"I feel the same way, sweetheart. You have been so supportive. I am lucky to have you."

"Don't mess with me; I am the lucky gal. Come here." She kissed me on my lips.

"I love you so much, Shanaya," I said from the bottom of my heart.

"I love you too, Nikhil."

Months later, on another autumn evening, I sat down on the comfy chair in my office, my legs wrapped around its bottom with the tip of a pen in my mouth. I felt exhausted. Reading the numerous emails from the suppliers and their price quotations made my head spin.

As I tapped my index finger on the mouse to move to the next mail, I saw my father walking towards me with a satisfactory smile on his face.

"Nikhil, I just had a word with your uncle. We are planning to send you and your cousin brother Nakul to Paris for an international conference at the end of this month," he announced as he pulled a chair and sat opposite me.

I stared at him open-mouthed.

"Really, Dad? You want me to go for a conference and that too in Paris?' I queried bewildered.

"Yes, since you have gained ample knowledge of the raw material and process here, I think it's the right opportunity and time for you. It's been six months already."

"If it is beneficial for our business, then sure I would like to go." I nodded.

"In the conference, there will be metal suppliers from all over the world and I want you to meet the existing clients and make some new ones as well. Furthermore, as you may have observed that our profit margins have been shrinking for a long time, this is our best shot to revive our company and formulate better deals. Hence bigger profits," he added as he crossed his arms over the table.

"Alright, Dad, from today itself I will fix meetings with the existing clients and will try to take appointments with the new ones," I continued, closing my computer screen.

"Certainly, do that, and let me know the response," he said as he stood up and walked out.

A mischievous smile swept my face at the thought of Paris. "Finally, a thing to look forward to now," I cried.

It was exhilarating for me as I thought about going to a foreign country for business, to meet new people, interact with them, and mature deals. From months now, I was going for chemotherapy on Monday, office the rest of the weekdays and German classes on weekends. It was monotonous.

Nothing seemed to excite me at all during these months, except Shanaya. Finally, digressing from my mundane and boring routine, a trip to Paris – the most romantic and beautiful city – made me feel all exuberant. The image of the Eiffel Tower came to my mind. I thought about its magnificence and beauty.

My uncle was a veteran in the scrap business. He was much more experienced than my father, and his son Nakul was just a couple of years elder to me. I thought that this trip would be a very good professional experience and also a recreational one with my brother. Nakul was a popular guy in college back in the day. Every time I met him, he always had a bunch of stories and a couple of hilarious blunders that had happened with his ex-girlfriends.

Seconds later, I dialled Shanaya's number on my phone as my fingers wiggled with excitement.

"Hi, Shanaya, guess what?"

"Umm. Did you tell your dad about me?" she giggled.

"Uh, no. That's not gonna happen soon."

"Umm... Aunty has invited me for lunch?"

"Oh, come on. I am going to Paris this month with Nakul for a business conference."

"Wow, really! I am so happy for you, pumpkin."

"Thank you. I am over my toes since the moment he told me."

"Congrats, Nikhil. Remember I told you that things will turn out well eventually. Your mother is absolutely fine now and you are getting an opportunity to attend your first international conference in Paris."

"You were so right. I was being pessimistic this whole time," I sprawled out. You have been the one lifting me up," I added as I got up from my chair with the phone pressed to my ear.

"Trust me, I am that optimistic only when it comes to you."

"I will remember that forever. Anyway, I will give you a call after dinner."

As the conversation ended, I caved into my chair again, thinking of what I could do there.

♋

For almost ten days, I had been tearing my hair all out surfing the internet for potential new clients, and trying to schedule meetings with them. As it was just a two-day convention, every company had a very stringent schedule. I called up several new companies that were participating in the event; many were from France, a few from Germany and others from Belgium. With the effective utilization of my foreign language skills of German and French to communicate with them, I arranged eight meetings.

My brother Nakul also scheduled some scrap yard visits for three days after the conference to purchase the material. We planned the trip for seven days, which included the two-day conference, a couple of days of yard visits, and the rest for leisure.

It took me almost six hours to finish my packing with the help of a list handed to me by Nakul. From a nail cutter to a hair conditioner, his list consisted of everything. I was glad he did not include porn on his master list.

The flight was scheduled to take off at eleven in the morning. I was wondering how I will survive the butterflies that were emerging from my stomach in excitement. I couldn't wait for the morning; I was literally bouncing off the walls.

Burned out, I lay in my king size bed when Enrique was setting up the mood for the commencement of the trip. Suddenly the song stopped and I heard buzzing. I turned around and picked up the phone. It was Shanaya.

"Hey, Nikhil," I heard as I pushed the phone to my ear.

"Hi."

"I am so excited that you are going for your first business conference. My pumpkin is growing now." She giggled.

"You know what, I still can't believe that I am really going," I retorted.

"I recommend you look at your tickets and visa again, then you will believe it," she chuckled.

"Oh, come on, what I meant was that it is actually incredible that finally, the day has come," I replied.

"Anyway, have you taken the basic medicines as it is difficult to get them there without prescription?"

"Yes, and I am well familiar with my stomach," I chuckled.

"Ha-ha. That was amazing." She mock laughed.

"Now some instructions from a possessive girlfriend of yours. No strip clubs and full-body massages," she instructed.

"Why not strip clubs?" I asked amused.

"Hmmm. I guess someone wants a little spanking," she said sarcastically. "Anyway, I know you will not be able to talk much, but at least be online on WhatsApp."

"Don't worry, I will be active."

♋

"Nikhil, wake up! Wake up! We have reached," my brother Nakul hollered repeatedly as he shook my shoulder.

I opened my eyes in a flash. My body felt lethargic, wishing to sleep for at least a couple of more hours.

"Finally, we have reached," I observed as I looked outside the airplane cabin window and saw the other big planes on the runway.

"Did you sleep well, bro?" Nakul asked with raised eyebrows.

"Oh yeah! Like an owl." I threw him a simper followed by a pout.

"What?"

"I was scared to death with the turbulence."

It was finally in the last hour of the flight when my mind finally gave up the ghost of fear and I slept watching *Friends*.

"Haha. Poor Nikhil. But I slept like a baby," he teased putting his hand on my shoulder.

"I know, as you were clinging to the bottle of chardonnay like a child does to his milk bottle."

"Oh, come on! I just had a couple of glasses. Anyway, let's go," he requested as he stood up from his seat.

I stretched myself before getting up from the seat. Damn! My back ached.

After collecting our luggage, we walked through the exit gate of the Charles de Gaulle airport, which is France's largest International airport. As soon as I stepped outside the gate, a breeze as cold as ice hit me and shook my bones. I unzipped my handbag, took out my woollen jacket and wore it.

We searched for our driver among the crowd at the exit gate.

"Hey, look Nakul, that's Benjamin. He is holding a nameplate with your name," I said pointing a finger towards the driver.

We walked towards him pulling our heavy luggage trolleys.

"Hi Benjamin, I am Nakul Gupta," he introduced himself forwarding his arm for a handshake.

"Bonjour Monsieur Gupta, Bienvenue en France. Welcome to France."

He wished both of us one by one with a smile.

He took the luggage trolleys and gestured at us to follow him to the parking.

On our way to our hotel, I pulled the window of the car down and welcomed the fresh chilly air running all over my face. It was eight in the evening and apart from the occasional noise of the honking cars, the city drew silent. The city roads looked so clean that I wished to walk barefeet on it sometime during the trip. I lay back on my seat, my eyes constant on the road trying to hold this moment deep down in my memory.

My mouth almost flew open when my eyes fell on the mesmerizing view of magnificent towers and buildings being an epitome of perfect incorporation of architecture and engineering.

"Bro, this city is marvellous. Check out the gorgeous architecture," I remarked.

"Wait for the Eiffel Tower. You will be awestruck with that giant magnificent wonder. I have read that it is visible from our hotel," he stated.

"Really?"

"Yes, and our room is on the nineteenth floor," he added.

"Incredible, I just can't wait." My voice grew louder as I spoke.

"Calm down! You will have ample of time to explore the city after the conference."

"Umm. You are right, I guess."

An hour later, Benjamin finally stopped the car. The name of the hotel was highlighted in blue.

It was Pullman Paris Montparnasse located in the heart of the city.

Benjamin rushed towards us as we got out.

"Mr Gupta, your luggage will be sent to your room."

Nakul nodded sliding his hand into his pocket and handed Benjamin a tip.

"Merci beaucoup, Monsieur," he thanked him.

We wished him goodbye with a smile and walked towards the reception.

The moment I pulled the big glass entrance door open, a gush of warm air enveloped me. Just outside the door, it was freakishly cold, and inside, thanks to the hotel central air conditioning, the temperature changed in the flash of a second.

As we walked straight, my eyes grasped the big vintage chandelier on the ceiling, probably containing more than one thousand bulbs working in a single unit. The lobby consisted of a conference room on the right, a restaurant and a big sitting area at the left.

Nakul went to complete the check-in formalities.

"Hello, my name is Nakul Gupta. We have a booking here," he said to the receptionist.

"Bonjour Monsieur; my name is Melanie. Please wait for a moment."

She was dressed in a shirt and knee length pencil skirt.

"Yes, sir. Sir, would you prefer two single beds or one king size bed if you are a couple?"

"Yeah. What? I am sorry?" Nakul responded. "We are brothers. Two single beds will be fine."

We both laughed at the thought of us being a couple.

"I am really sorry, sir," she replied embarrassed, her cheeks turning pink.

♋

Still laughing, we entered our room on the nineteenth floor in ecstasy. The moment Nakul put the hotel card into the wall holder, light illuminated our room.

The room, excessively spacious, consisted of two big single beds with a couple of small cushions, an enormous LCD TV on the front wall, with a very beautiful painting of the French revolution at the back of the beds. A set of round wooden tables with two overstuffed single seated couches were placed in front of the giant glass window on the right side of the beds.

We inched forward and kept our handbags on the bed.

"Nikhil, come here look at this view," Nakul called as he drew the curtains from the window.

I scurried towards the window, and saw the great Eiffel Tower as bright as the moon in front of me, the lights marvelously lighting it, distinguishing it from the contiguous buildings and towers. As I looked at it, I was flushed by the panoramic view of the entire city. I stood rooted to the spot for minutes. The Seine River ran next to the tower. After taking a shower, we both went to the conference area to confirm our participation.

♋

Next morning, parched and edgy, I grabbed the water bottle from the side table outside the conference area in the hotel lobby. I was gulping another sip when I noticed a foreigner from the corner of my eye, sitting quietly on the black leather couch staring at his phone's screen. I momentarily looked on the name tag that all the participants had been given.

My eyes brightened up as I saw the company name. The executive was from STR Germany. I had been after this company for months as it was one of the biggest aluminium scrap companies which produced thousands of tons of aluminium every month. I had also tried to arrange a meeting, but I was unsuccessful as they were not entertaining new clients.

I kept the empty bottle on the side table and darted towards the supplier. To impress him, I decided to communicate in German with him.

"Entschuldigen Sie bitte." (Excuse me.)

"Ja." (Yes.) He folded his hands on his lap.

"Können wir bitte Visitenkarten austauschen?" (Can we please exchange business cards?)

"Gewiß, greifen Sie bitte einen Sitz," (Certainly, please grab a seat), he said while shaking my hand.

We exchanged our business cards.

"Hi, Nikhil, I am Jose Brown from STR Germany. We deal in all types of Aluminum scrap," he said while adjusting his black tie with his right hand.

After the introduction, we started talking about the material and price.

I meticulously looked at each and every picture of the material while zooming in and out, and constantly trying to get a closer look. I checked it over and over again as it would be my first deal and I didn't want to mess it up. We exchanged few prices and negotiated over it for a few minutes.

"1600$/metallic ton done final price," I offered him a price.

He stared at my face as he rubbed his knuckles. His forehead furrowed.

"It's not a good price for me, but I have a gut feeling that we can expand our relationship in the future. Deal?" he said mischievously with a smile on his face as he forwarded his hand for a handshake.

"Deal," I shook hands with him.

He noted the material quantity and price on his mini notepad along with my company name.

"I will send you the contract in a couple of days and then you can make the advance payment."

"Sure thing," I replied.

"Are you visiting Germany after the conference? I can show some other material from our yards," he asked adjusting the lapels of his coat.

"Not this time. I have some yard visits scheduled in France, but I will definitely visit soon," I responded, pinching the bridge of my nose.

He nodded and said, "It was nice doing business with you, Nikhil, and I am amazed that you speak Deutsch so fluently."

"Thank you very much."

"*Tschus!*" (Bye!) I replied, ending the conversation in German.

After the deal, I was feeling confident as I had managed to get such a big client from Germany with the help of my language skills. My father's words echoed in my brain, "Education is the only thing which no one can take away from you."

And that day I realized what he actually meant, as I had not wanted to continue with my classes earlier, but he had persuaded me to continue.

"My feet are just killing me right now. What about you, Nakul?" I whined while stretching my legs straight on the bed, fatigued by the continuous meetings.

"I am exhausted too. Let's rest for some time and then we will go to Pizza Roma. I searched it online, it's just five miles away from the hotel," he said while putting his hands over his head in a folded position to relax and crossed his legs.

"Oh really, that sounds delicious! I am famished already," I responded, my eyebrows raised.

"Yeah! But before that, let's smoke a Cuban cigar. I bought it from the Delhi Airport and as long as we are on foreign land, it doesn't count," he proposed.

"Yes, I want to try that." I turned my head towards him.

He got up from the bed, grabbed his handbag and took out a matchbox and one cigar, which had a plastic yellowish filter.

"Wow, this is incredible; these Cubans, I tell you, are the best ones in the world."

He pressed his lips on the cigar and sucked in closing his eyes. He blew out the rich benignant cigar smoke through his chest. He puffed again and this time the smoke came out in the form of rings.

"It's my turn now," I said with an excited face.

With the cigar pressed between my lips, I inhaled the smoke. My chest was now fluffed. Suddenly I coughed out the smoke from my mouth. I felt uncomfortable.

"It happens, bro, since you are trying it for the first time; try again, but slowly this time," he said empathetically.

I sucked a cluster of air from the yellow filter and didn't cough out the smoke this time. After a few consecutive drags, my head tossed and body eased as the seconds passed.

"I feel so sluggish right now, nice stuff," I complimented, passing a smile.

"These are the best; I always buy them when I am travelling," he chuckled.

Minutes later, tossed by the Cuban tobacco, I got up from the bed and took out my casual wear from the suitcase and changed.

Nakul and I walked out of the hotel. He waved his hand towards the first taxi that approached us as we were too tired to walk five miles. A gray coloured Toyota Prius stopped in front of us. Surprisingly, Toyota, being a Japanese brand, captured more market in Paris than other European cars.

"Pizza Roma on Montparnasse street," Nakul informed the driver.

"Definitely, sir. Please be seated," he replied in return, beckoning us to take our seats with his eyes.

My breath almost ceased as my eyes glanced at the pay-meter. The meter ticked from the base price of eighteen Euros, which was far more expensive than Delhi, and with each mile, the fare incremented with a minimum of two euro. My head initiated the computation for the final price. Damn! We should have walked instead, my subconscious dipped in frugality hollered.

After paying a hefty amount of thirty Euros, we entered Pizza Roma. The restaurant was jam-packed, but luckily, we found a corner window table at the right end. We walked quickly and sat down. The restaurant had wooden tables draped red tablecloths and big couches and a well-festooned bar that richly demonstrated more than fifteen varieties of wine. Then I saw a couple enjoying their delicious pizza. My mouth watered and I licked my lips.

And then I saw a French family, a middle-aged couple with a teenage son, smoking cigarettes together. Apparently, the family was open about their habits and the fact that they were so comfortable about smoking together blew my mind away.

After a while, a handsome man in white bakery uniform wearing a baker's hat approached us.

"Bonsoir Monsieur. This is the complimentary bread basket and the menu. Enjoy your evening." He smiled as he kept a hand-woven braided bread basket on our table and handed the menus.

"Très bien, merci," (thank you) I replied.

"Could you please get us two glasses of red wine?" I asked.

"In a minute," the waiter said and left.

The basket contained the famous Croissant, half French Loaf, Baguette and the Brioche along with a portion of butter. I rubbed my hands excitedly; my stomach growled. I had heard before, that eating a butter and cheese croissant with a cup of coffee in a French café is considered a top rated cultural experience.

"Wipe your drool, Nikhil, wait!" He grabbed the black vinegar and olive oil bottle from the cutlery holder kept on the right end of the table and poured it one by one on the quarter plate.

He mixed the combo with his index finger.

"Dip the bread, it will taste delicious," he suggested.

"Okay," I nodded quickly.

I picked the croissant and skimmed it over the assortment and ate it.

"Yummy! It tastes awesome. Nakul."

I was joyful by the gesture of this Italian restaurant making its customers feel special and wanted.

As the first sip of my Cabernet Franc red wine mingled into my saliva, my taste buds went euphoric. Smooth and refreshingly delicious, it reminded me of one saying: 'Wine makes daily living easier, less hurried, with fewer tensions and more tolerance.'

Pleased, I gazed at the streets. It was quite surprising that all the cafes and restaurants were all along the street.

At 9.30 p.m., people were walking down the streets in good number. Every other girl on the street was gorgeous and stylishly dressed. No wonder it was called one of the most fashionable cities in the world. Even in the thrashing cold, they were wearing short dresses. I wondered what summer would be like! Only if one could know what was running in my mind.

I missed Shanaya at that point. How nice it would have been to share this beautiful evening in Paris with her.

"Bro, this city is intoxicating. With this cold weather, lovely ambience and beautiful girls, I don't think I would ever want to go home now." Overawed in the moment, I was chuffed to bits.

"Ha-ha. You are such a smug. But I can't ignore the fact that this is amazing."

I opened the two-page menu and started my quest for the most delicious pizza. It extravagantly boasted numerous choices in vegetarian and meat pizzas.

Suddenly my eyes spotted a gorgeous, tall and a voluptuous girl walking inside the restaurant, wearing a wine-coloured backless dress. Her brown ruffled long hair and the luminous eyes and crimson cheeks added flavour to her beauty.

'Holy crap! Can anyone be more beautiful than her?' My brain queried as I shook my head.

And my heart returned quickly with the obvious 'Shanaya'.

As I continued staring at her, her eyes rolled at me for a second. I shook my head in embarrassment. Damn! This is so awkward! I uttered.

"Did you check out that red wine?" his mouth gaped.

"As the matter of fact, I did. So, are we calling her red wine now?" I put my arms on the table.

"I want to drink that red wine," he said burying his hands in his hair.

"You pervert, order your pizza please," I giggled slapping him on the arm.

"I am going to ask her out." He leaned back on his seat.

"Go and get yourself kicked in the crotch. You prick, can't you see that she has joined that big group?" I said pointing my eyes towards her.

"Shit, my bad luck," he said with a gentle kick on the floor as he turned his head and looked at the girl again.

"Never mind bro. Better luck next time," I joked with a sardonic smile on my face.

"Anyway, cheers to one heck of a city!" he said while raising his glass and making eye contact.

"Cheers to Paris!" I exclaimed as we clinked our wine glasses together.

"Cheers to smoking, hot girls, and one night stands!" He cried out louder this time, raising his glass again.

After treating our stomachs with delectable pizza and savoury red wine – the alcoholic beverage of course, not the girl – we went straight to our hotel in the cab as it was already late. I retired to my bed, all worn out.

♋

"Hey, Nakul! How come people are leaving early today? It's just five in the evening," I asked as we crossed paths the next day in the lobby outside the conference area.

"As you know international metal prices are on all time high since the past one week and the market is very volatile." He gulped a few sips of water from the water bottle. "The buyers as well as the sellers both want to wait and let the market stabilize." He plucked at the cuff of his shirt.

"Yeah! Even I could not buy any cheap material today, but made many new contacts."

I was more confident the second day about myself and sensed self-confidence building in myself during all meetings that had happened.

"Many suppliers have morning flight tomorrow, so they are going to tour Paris."

"I am done with my meetings. Going to rest in the room for some time."

"Sure. I will catch up in an hour." His voice came in a murmur as he walked away.

♋

"Wow! This feels incredible!" I exclaimed with joy while stretching my legs and hands wide on the most comfortable bed I have ever laid on. I moved towards the side table and grasped a glass of wine. As I took a couple of sips, I could feel my nerves calming down. I grabbed my phone from my coat's pocket and video called Shanaya on Facetime. Luckily, she picked after a few buzzes.

"Hey!" I yelled smiling exposing my teeth.

Her face glowed the moment she saw me on her phone's screen. She was wearing light gray T-shirt and loose pyjamas. She looked extremely beautiful under the shadow of her natural glow. I had missed her so much in these couple of days.

"Hi pumpkin, how are you?" she asked as she sat on her bed combing her hair with her hands. Her room, as usual, was untidy with clothes and shoes strewn around. As far as I knew her, she must have returned from somewhere.

"I am good. Did you just come back from somewhere?"

"Yeah, I went out with my friends for lunch and just came back."

"I knew it from the moment I saw the pile of clothes behind you," I tittered.

"You know me very well, mister," she said and winked.

"Anyway, I matured my first deal yesterday." I shrugged.

"Congrats! That's awesome, Nikhil. I am so proud of you." Her eyes lightened up.

"Thanks a lot," I responded.

"So this is your room, it is so spacious and beautiful, and the painting over your head, so breathtaking."

"I like this painting so much that I think I might take it back to India," I jested.

"It will look great in your room, I must say."

"Anyway, I really want you here with me right now. I wish I could cuddle with you here on this big bed." I ran my hand on the mattress.

"Oh really, and what else?" she asked mischievously while raising her eyebrow.

"I would love to kiss you on your lips while swaying my tongue all over your body and bite you like a KitKat. Do you want me to remove my shirt?" I asked biting my lower lip, my eyes narrowed.

"Umm," she moaned as her lower lip trembled, her eyes wide. "Go on, please. Well, my T-shirt is very itchy and this bra too," she replied as she pulled her T-shirt down from the middle, exposing her cleavage.

I unclasped my shirt button one by one, removing it completely while gazing at her, my eyes fixed and intense, my lips curled into my mouth.

"I am sure you will take off your pants as well."

"Only if you want me to," I replied with my hands on my zip now.

"Ohh, I would love that!"

"Nikhil, wait! I am sorry but my mother is just outside the room. I was kidding!" she screamed.

"Fuck! You gave me a boner this time. Don't play with me, woman."

"I wish I was with you in Europe, especially Paris; it is so breathtakingly beautiful," she blurted with a big smile on her face.

"I forgot to tell you. Nakul and I will be going to Queen Club on Champs Élysées street tonight."

"That's good, have fun there and don't dance with French girls."

"Oh, come on, what's the harm in a little dancing and flirting."

"What?" Her face turned red.

"Sorry, I was just messing with you. Look at your face, Shanaya," I cackled.

"Okay. A little dance is fine. Be in your limits, Mr Gupta, or else I will punch and spank you hard when you come back."

"Okay okay."

"Definitely and I will be watching you from here like a hawk." She laughed.

"Ha-Ha. Shit, now I have to be careful, good night."

♋

"Nikhil, can you see all these beautiful, smoking hot girls or is it just me? I guess it is raining angels in this city," Nakul chattered.

"What, say that again? I couldn't hear you," I inched towards his face.

"I said the girls are too beautiful here," he returned curving a hand near my ear and repeated himself.

"If you say so, bro." I took another mouthful of my fourth drink of single malt, cold and icy, slightly sweet and tasty against my lips, as I always drank whiskey with coke. I held the drink in my mouth for a brief moment and allowed the ice and the whiskey to rest on my taste buds. It was clear in my mind that I was soon going to be very drunk.

To get through the stag entry, we had to take a cover charge of over two hundred Euros, which pierced a big hole in my pocket.

The music was loud and the club was full of amateurs dancing and drinking alcohol, as if there was no tomorrow. It was enormous, containing the capacity of over six hundred people. The dance floor particularly was gigantic and the tables and the couches were laid across the walls in the corners. Multicoloured flashing lights flashed repeatedly on the completely jam-packed dance floor over people's faces and clothes, with the house music being played.

I was in my favourite black T-shirt with Deutschland written on it with bold red letters, which was gifted by my sister, and my blue jeans.

With a faint view, I saw a group of teenagers across the bar betting for money about who could down the maximum number of beer mugs in two minutes. I experienced the thumping voice of the buffer getting synchronized with my heartbeat. Nakul gestured to the bartender. "One Vodka shot please!" he mouthed, and the bartender nodded and disappeared into the cries of a hundred other thirsty youngsters.

As I finished my fourth drink, my bladder felt like bursting. I pushed back the tall chair and stood up to go to the restroom. I staggered through the crowd and finally reached the restroom.

"Boy, I guess the real party is here!" I said to myself. The scene inside was beyond belief. Young boys and girls were lying on the floor. I stood at my spot with a face of a freak and continued staring. One boy meticulously drew a straight line of a white powder drug, probably cocaine or Mary Jane(Marijuana) on the back of a topless girl bent down across the floor, while the other rolled a twenty euro note into a perfectly cylindrical shape and sniffed. He tweaked his nostrils followed by a long sigh.

I took in a heavy breath and glanced around when I saw a few juvenile couples half naked, probably drunk and making out, caring for nobody around.

After relieving myself, I walked back to the bar counter, making my way again through the enthusiastic crowd.

I noticed Nakul sitting with a girl on my seat at the bar with a figure hugging short red dress barely covering her privates. She wore very light make-up and dark red lipstick. Boy! She was hard to miss. No wonder Nakul found her. I chose not to disturb him and went to the other end of the bar.

I waved to the bartender and shouted, "One Jack Daniels with a coke please!" I was a little dizzy, but I wanted to get happy high; after all, you don't get many chances to get drunk in Paris.

Soon, I was left standing alone with a drink in my hand near the dance floor when I saw an average height, lean, and in all probability, a French girl coming towards me. As she kept coming closer, I couldn't help but notice how she was dressed up to the nines in her brown boots, looking stunning in a black cocktail thigh length dress, sticking a cigarette in her pink lips and messing up her tidy hair with her hands. The dress covered her breasts partially.

"Bonjour," she initiated.

I was dumbstruck with her blue eyes flashing at me and mind failed to register what she said.

"Bonjour," I replied hastily, nervously staring with cow's eyes, thinking that's what she probably would have said.

"Do you have a lighter?" The cigarette hung immobile in her mouth.

"Umm..." I put my hands into my pockets, searching for a lighter in reflex, although I knew I didn't have one.

"Sorry." I shrugged.

"Okay, let me check again, are you from India?" she enquired as she searched through her bag for a lighter.

"Why? Yes." I responded. "My name is Nikhil Gupta," I said extending my hand towards her for a gentle handshake.

"I am Blair, nice to meet you Nikhil,' she replied with a playful smile and kept her cigarette inside her purse.

"Pleasure is all mine," I retorted as a smile travelled up my face.

"I am guessing you have many Indian friends. Are you a student or working around here?" I asked inquisitively after pausing for a moment.

"I am learning baking from Le Cordon Bleu and I have few Indian friends there, who I think are very nice." She kept her right hand on her waist and constantly twirled her hair with the other.

"Oh! That's the best bakery school in the whole of Europe, I think. Glad to know you know about Indian people. Also, I am sure you bake well," I said sarcastically, instantly wondering why the hell had I just said that. Trying not to feel guilty, I blamed it on the liquor because I didn't have the guts to say something like that to a girl, not even in my untamed dreams.

Before I could come back with an apology, she corrected, "I know you don't mean that, but as a matter of fact, I am." She passed a slow and sexy smile.

"And yes, I know a lot of people from India, and they can't all be nice. But I felt you are," she remarked.

Brains with beauty, I couldn't help but juggle the thoughts in my head about it being a sign of flirtation or her just being polite. I inhaled a deep breath and blew out slowly.

Quickly sensing my drifting thoughts, she interrupted, "And you?"

"I am here for a business trip and it's my first time in Europe."

"That's great. Holy crap! I'd like to chat more, but this is my favourite song. Would you like to dance?" she asked casually.

"I don't see a reason why not," I said passing a smile.

'Oh my god! You are too stoned Nikhil, you are going to regret this!' My subconscious warned me. I was actually drunk, but I thought it was just dancing; not a big deal. It's good to make friends outside your country. At least that is what I thought I was doing, making a friend. I was curious to see how this would end.

I took her hand in mine and sauntered to the dance floor, making our way to the middle while dismembering the crowd. People were swaying madly in complete rhythm to the music.

On the floor, Blair kept her hand around my neck over my shoulders and my hands unwittingly glided down her back. Her dress felt soft and a shiver ran down my body as I looked back at her.

My head tossed once again, thanks to Mr Jack Daniels and the ear-splitting music which echoed in my ear. I felt the moment taking over me. Just when I tried holding back, she started with her moves, taking me along with her, her body swaying to music. I could sense that she was a tremendous dancer. She turned elegantly, her body in tune with the fast music. My heartbeat was growing steadily along with it.

She raised her soft curved arms to the escalating beat. Her blue feline eyes took me far away from the club to a euphoric island. I was on the edge of paradise.

Her dress slipped down one shoulder, and in reflex, I looked away. Without noticing her dress, she held my face and turned it towards her while she worked her fingers through her hair.

She was staring into my eyes, as if trying to hypnotize me, as I couldn't feel my body anymore and my head was definitely not in its place. Her hands were now on my back and I was skimming her waist line. I was going with the flow, thinking that since I was completely under the influence of alcohol, it was alright.

She whirled abruptly and dashed into the oblivion of the night. Her bottom touched my thighs. A spark ran all over my body. I took a deep breath, my nostrils flared. Her body had a gripping fragrance of an expensive rose perfume blended with her natural essence. Our bodies moved together as the beat progressed and then again, she turned swiftly. I ran a finger over her cleavage. Being sunk in the moment, my lower lip quivered. Her chest rose and fell with quick breaths. She drew closer and licked her lips. We continued dancing for another twenty minutes.

"You dance so well," she whispered.

"I think you are the one who is making me dance like this," I swallowed nervously.

"Don't say that!" She pressed her finger on my lips, raised her chin and planted a kiss on my neck. "Let's get this party going to my place."

What the hell! What am I doing? This is so wrong, I growled inside my head as I heard her words.

She sensed the throbbing nerve on my forehead.

"It's okay if you don't want to. We can continue dancing," she said with disappointment.

"Geez, Umm. it's not like that," I stammered. Words failed me.

"Actually, I have the morning flight to India tomorrow and I have to go back to my hotel as my brother must be waiting," I mumbled as I darted closer to her ear.

I lied, making an excuse. I felt as if Shanaya was watching. I was embarrassed as I hadn't stopped it earlier. Damn! I feel like I just cheated on her!

"Nikhil, can't you squeeze in an hour? My place is very close to this club," she said with her hands now cupping my hip. She was breathing hard. I took a step back from her firm grip.

I glanced at my wrist watch as if I was checking out the time and said, "I am really sorry, Blair, I can't stay now; it's getting late. But I would like to be in touch, If you'd like," I said trying to end the conversation.

"I wish you could spend the night. Anyway, dial your number from my phone here, and give a missed call," she said as her face muscles loosened up.

"Thank you."

I took her phone and saved my number on her cell phone as 'Nikhil (India)'.

I gave her phone back and leaned towards her to give a goodbye hug.

"Goodnight, Nikhil, it was a pleasure meeting you."

"Same here Blair, and do share one of your recipes," I giggled.

"Damn! You are so good at this," she said with an open mouth smile.

"As in?" I asked with raised eyebrows

"You are a charmer, Nikhil."

"You would be surprised to know that you are the first one to say that to me, Blair."

"Well, there you go. I am that first."

She pressed her lips to my cheek, ran her finger on my neck and left.

I suddenly saw Nakul walking towards me at the bar.

"Where the hell were you, Nikhil?" he demanded.

"I am sorry, bro. I met someone and I completely lost track of time," I answered mockingly as he was talking to a girl earlier and I was the one who had given them privacy.

"It's okay, you're my brother and I want you to have fun," he said sipping his drink, with a smirk.

"You look pale, didn't have fun? Did she leave you?" I questioned.

"Please don't ask."

"Why not?"

"She was so drunk that she puked over my shoes," he said embarrassingly.

"OMG! She didn't! I can't believe I had a better time than you," I simpered keeping my hands on his shoulders. I laughed so much that my stomach ached.

"I would appreciate a little empathy here," he begged.

"You got to be kidding me. Empathize with you and leave my only chance to give it back to you?"

"What about you?"

"We danced and then she invited me to her place."

"And?" he asked with his mouth wide open.

"I stepped back; it would have been wrong, and you know I love Shanaya."

"Hmm, never mind," he replied.

"Let's go now; we have a morning train to catch for the yard visits."

We left the club and went back to our hotel. My head was spinning the whole time. I took an oath to myself to never drink like a fish again.

Deep down in my stomach, I was feeling shameful for what I had done. No one could have loved me the way she did and I had almost risked it for nothing, I thought, shaking my head. A desperate prayer flew from my heart, thanking god that nothing more than a casual dance had happened.

♋

For the next three days, we travelled to various parts of France in the TGV (Train à Grande Vitesse) train connecting different parts of Europe as well, which are France's high speed trains.

We visited all the scrap yards from Nord-Pas-de-Calais-Picardie in the north of France to Languedoc-Roussillon-Midi-Pyrénées, in the south. I ended up making long term business relations with some of the companies I met as I spoke to them comfortably in French.

While travelling, I observed that some states in France were greener and lot less inhabited than Paris, symbolizing less industrialization.

The most important factors shouldering my frugality were the food and taxi fares; they were cheaper everywhere in France apart from Paris, which was the most extravagant. I also observed a large population of African Americans, who had become residents and citizens of France, some as students and others as temporary workers. According to my brother, they were descendants of people earlier brought over to fight in World War I.

After the three-day hectic tour, we finally returned to Paris in the evening. As soon as I reached my room, I poured myself a glass of red wine. I had one more day left to explore the city tomorrow, so I decided to go to the Eiffel Tower that night itself as I wanted to see the view from the top in the dark. My brother Nakul said he'd pass as he was weary and he had already seen it before.

♋

As I stepped out of the cab, my face awestruck with the beauty of one of the seven wonders of the world, my jaw went slack. The iron giant was magnificently crafted and was sparkling with thousands of light bulbs.

I scurried towards the giant and noticed that there was no security or checkpoints near the tower, unlike monuments in India. Here, it was just like walking through a playing field. I found children playing football near the tower.

At the ticket counter, I found myself in the queue next to almost twenty people. There was also an option to climb the Eiffel Tower up the stairs, but lazy bones me preferred the lift.

Finally, up many levels of elevators, I reached the top. And as the door opened, my mouth gaped and a muscle in my jaw clenched.

The view was extraordinarily gorgeous. The tower lay beside the Seine River. One could easily see the reflection of the moon and the stars in it, adding to the panoramic view from the Eiffel Tower.

God! I missed Shanaya so much at that moment. I would have been in seventh heaven if she would have been here with me. I wished to hold her hands and take her in my arms and share this moment with her. The entire city looked like the sky with scintillating stars and satellites. Words failed me as I closed my eyes and tried to capture a mental image of this moment, keeping it safe in my brain for the rest of my life.

The next morning, Nakul and I decided to explore the streets of the city and buy a few gifts for everyone back home. As we stepped outside the hotel, my eyes sighted tumultuous, dark, ragged clouds. The icy north wind blew the snowflakes right into our faces. The sudden chill brought my eyes back to earth and I saw that there was snow. It was the first time in my life I had seen snowfall.

It was colder than expected, even though we had layered ourselves with heavy woolen clothing. My bones shivered and my teeth chattered. I wrapped my arms around myself.

I found it difficult to stroll around in the cold. Later, as we continued walking down the streets, luckily, we found the Lafayette Gallery near the adjoining street from the hotel.

"Let's go in there Nakul," I suggested pointing my finger towards it.

He nodded and we entered. My eyes widened and I frowned glancing towards the magnificent complex consisting of the most expensive brands like Louis Vuitton, Hermes, etc.

"Nakul, I don't think I can buy anything from here," I laughed.

"Let's go in, there is no harm in window shopping."

With a heavy heart, I started browsing through the shops. It housed mostly luxury brands.

The clothes there were way more expensive than any other part of Paris. It was then that we decided to seek out the local street shops.

After a painstaking quest, we found out a couple of good, reasonable shops along the street. One thing that took me by surprise was the quality of the material. It was of superior quality but significantly cheaper. I purchased a couple of woollen overcoats for Shanaya, a few jumpsuits for my sister, and some sweaters for my parents.

In the late afternoon, after we were done with the shopping, the sun rose in a blended combination of cherry and gold, splitting light all over the snowy land and the white clouds. From a chilly morning, it evolved into a pleasant day as the sun jumped to its zenith. We had just finished a beautiful long walk when we decided to go for a leisure cruise on the Seine River. It was a one hour cruise on the river throughout the heart of Paris. On board, we enjoyed the audio commentary that spoke of the the Parisian culture in both English and French and soaked in the view of splendid Parisian structures, picturesque bridges and historical monuments like The Louvre and Grand Palais exhibition hall. We also explored a museum that offered a complimentary lunch.

Later in the evening, we treated our taste buds with one last scrumptious meal in Paris. I wouldn't have missed it for the world; my last chance to eat the whole bread basket and pizza at Pizza Roma.

After dinner, we walked out again in the freezing cold, our hands shoved tightly in our jacket pockets. The gentle shaking of my bones continued.

"God! The cold is overwhelming," I wailed.

As we turned through the corner on the street, our eyes fell on a strip club called Mad Horse. Amazed, we stopped for a moment and then gazed towards the entrance.

It had a big transparent glass display area just adjacent to the entrance door. There were three girls in bikinis dancing around the pole in front of each of them while looking towards the people walking on the street.

My eyes flashed wide open with the view as it was so openly displayed on the street. One of the strippers locked my gaze and waved her long finger at me seductively as her body slid across the pole, and then rolled it back, insinuating me to come inside.

"Would you like to go in?" Nakul asked with a smirk, as his eyeballs fixed on the girl at the middle.

"I will pass," I returned nodding my head as I had already done one stupid thing on this trip.

"Oh, come on! Let's just check out this place. What's the big deal?"

I was firm in my decision of not going inside, but didn't want to stop Nakul, so I suggested, "I will take a cab and go back to the hotel. You go and have fun. Just remember we have a morning departure at 8 a.m., so we have to leave our hotel by five."

"Chuck it! I am not going alone," he said and started walking again.

Soon we reached our hotel and started packing. Finally it was done. My feet ached as I had walked miles in the freaking cold. I disconnected my phone from charging and typed Shanaya's number on the keypad with a smile on my face.

"Hey, I have been on my toes since morning, waiting for your call. You would have been in dark soup if you had not called me tonight," she hollered the moment I pressed the phone to my ear.

"Hi. Calm down! I missed you," I whined.

"Hmm. Then it's fine," she exhaled. "Anyway, how was your day?"

"It was great. We shopped and roamed around the streets on foot, exploring the city and then we went for a cruise on the Seine."

"Cruise! That's sounds amazing."

"It was indeed. I have bought macaroons for you."

"Oh! That sounds awesome. Thanks."

"My pleasure. Anyway, I will reach Delhi by 8 p.m. as I have a connecting flight and a two-hour halt at Abu Dhabi. So can we meet the day after tomorrow?"

"Yes, you know, my parents are going out of station for three days, so you can come to my place. We can spend some time together."

Alone time with her at her home; I was excited.

"Are you sure? What about your brother?"

"He will be in his office."

"It will be fun! Are you going to cook me something then?" I asked laughingly.

"Ha-ha. You wish," she replied mischievously.

"You must be tired, Nikhil. You should sleep now; I don't want you to miss your flight tomorrow."

"That sounds about right, good night."

As I disconnected the phone, I closed my eyes. I was so tired that I could not even feel my legs. I covered myself with the soft quilt imagining myself in Shanaya's warm, soft and comforting arms. God! That felt perfect.

♋

"Holy crap! My back and neck are hurting. How do you manage to sleep in the flight, Nakul?" I whined untying my shoes as a desperate attempt to make myself comfortable.

"I like being in the air and the turbulence excites me," he replied as he stretched his hands.

"I hope to be like you one day, the wavering makes me nauseous." I laughed.

The seat belt sign was switched on now. I inferred that we had reached Delhi.

In Paris, we had reached the airport well on time because of which I was able to spend some time in the duty-free shop. I grabbed a handful of Lindt chocolates and a couple of perfumes before boarding the flight.

My body cringed because it was lacking sleep. I stretched myself in vain. My eyes strained as I watched a couple of movies on the flight monitor.

I prayed god to let the landing be safe. The plane shook as its tyres skidded to a halt on the tarmac. Finally, we landed in Delhi. I gasped in relief.

On my way home, I texted Shanaya that I had reached Delhi.

♋

In front of the giant wooden door at the entrance of my house, I stood on my toes and pressed the doorbell with my index finger.

My sister's voice and footsteps could be heard approaching the door.

"Nikhil! Come on in!" she roared extending her arms wide as her mouth turned into a smile.

I quickly inched forward and was enveloped in a hug.

"Missed you, sis," I murmured.

We drew apart and tramped towards our parents' room.

"Hi, Mom and Dad," I screamed with a wave of excitement on my face.

They turned their faces towards me with huge smiles, seated on the bed.

"Welcome back, the apple of my eye," Mom greeted me.

I hugged Mom, planting a kiss on her cheek.

"We are so happy that you are back, son," my father added as I squeezed him tight in my arms.

"How was the trip?"Intrigued with the smile on my face, my mother asked.

"It was great, Mom, the conference went well, and we managed to go sightseeing in our free time. Paris is a very beautiful city," I asserted.

"I am glad that you had so much fun," Dad said patting my shoulder.

"Mom, I am craving for your handmade food today," I said sitting on the bed between them.

"I will definitely be the chef for my boy."

We all sat together on the bed as I described my trip. With Dad, I discussed all the business contracts that I had matured. Nikita and Mom asked about my experiences in France. I told them everything and Nikita became very excited and decided she would also plan a trip to Paris with her friends. And then I unclasped my suitcase and gave everyone the presents that I had bought.

After having a delightful dinner cooked by my mother, I lay on my bed. My stomach ached as I had eaten too much. While I was massaging my stomach with my hands, my phone rang. It was Shanaya.

"Hey! Finally, you are back, bravo!" she exclaimed as I put on the headphones to my ear.

"Hi, I just can't wait to meet you tomorrow."

"Nikhil, first tell me what shall we have for lunch?"

"Let's order north Indian food, but I am craving for you more. I just want to grab you in my arms tomorrow and kiss you for a very long time."

"Really?"

"Yeah, baby! Will eat you for lunch."

"Whatever do you mean mister, you are not gonna get it," she tittered.

"Whatever do you mean miss, we will see," I replied laughing.

We went on and on for hours till the time our bodies automatically dozed off to sleep. I told her about my experiences in France; their food, culture, some enlightening incidents during my business meetings. I told her about the strip club too. She said that I did the right thing by not going in. As far as the unbecoming dance with Blair in Queen Club was concerned, I decided to tell her face to face the next day. In case she got angry, I could apologize in person and could make her understand that it was a mistake.

ත

It was almost twelve and I was running late.

As I drove, my mind felt peculiarly twitchy. Maybe it was because of the fact that we would be alone for the first time like this. I had bought her favourite flowers – red carnations. I always treasured the smile on her flushed face whenever she brought the bouquet close to her nose to smell the flowers.

I parked my car a couple of houses away from her home. In the rear-view mirror, I admired my perfect spiked hair, my dark blue v-necked t-shirt, and black jeans. I looked handsome.

At her door, I rang the doorbell. Her footsteps could be heard coming towards the door in a rushed manner.

In a swift manner, she opened the door. My eyeballs stood still and my heart passed a breathless smile. She wore a white and blue striped shirt and hazy-blue saggy denims. Her face shimmered as she looked into my eyes and a smile grew on her lips, as wide as the ocean. Her eyebrows drooped, a muscle in her jaw clutched, she looked down the floor shying away from my unnerving gaze. Her cheeks crimson and soft, her lips moist, I continued gawking at the most beautiful chocolate brown eyes on the planet.

"Come in, please. You can stare at me later," she said bringing me out of my stupor and winked.

I nodded.

"These flowers are for you," I said as I handed the bouquet to her.

She smelled the flowers while leaning on the table.

I stepped in and rammed the door close behind. I extended my arms wide for a cuddle and she came in, clasping tightly to my body.

"I missed you so much," I whispered, taking a deep breath, my arms on her back.

"Thanks for the flowers. I want you for the rest of my life, Nikhil Gupta."

"You already stole my heart. What else is left, darling?" I planted a kiss on her forehead holding her face with my hands and we parted. With our gazed fixed, we stared at each other, completely baffled.

She stood still; her gaze was unwavering while the muscles on her face tightened.

Inching forward, I kept my lips on hers and licked her tongue, while pushing her towards the wall.

Her mouth gaped and my tongue slid deeper into her mouth. She reciprocated as she wrapped her hands around me.

"What do you have in mind, mister?" she whispered, biting her lower lip, her head tilted to the right and one eyebrow raised.

"I want to eat these scrumptious lips," I growled.

"Just the lips?" she asked chewing her lips.

I took her palms in mine and stretched it together upwards, touching the wall, and bit a large portion of her neck.

"Ouch!" She jumped on her feet and tried to get her hand out of my grip.

My tongue whirled over her underarms as I pushed my lower body onto hers. She panted, her eyes blinking like an owl. Now my tongue travelled to her right ear and I released her hands against the wall. I put my lips again on hers and my hands went massaging her butt in a circular motion. Boy! Her ass was smooth as velvet. Fascinated, she kept her hands on my chest, fondling the dark curls.

"You have beautiful hair, Shanaya," I held her hair in my hand, admiring their softness over my fingers, and watching the tresses tumble down.

My mouth was close to her ear and I took a long breath, sniffing her heavenly body fragrance.

She smiled up at me through her dark eye-lashes. Gently, I ran my hands upwards from her knee over her jeans.

"Woo! What are you doing to me, Nikhil?"

"You are mine, Shanaya. I love you," I groaned.

I leaned back and undid her first button of her shirt. Edging forward, I planted a kiss on her cleavage. With infinite slowness, I unclasped all the buttons as she trembled like a fish out of water. Her breast popped out from her pink brassiere.

My hands cupped her breasts. Soft and swollen, I squeezed and massaged them. She moaned in pleasure with an unconscious movement of her tongue.

"I love you so much, Nikhil. Please be with me for the rest of my life." She shuddered and hugged me tightly.

"I am all yours. Let's go to your room," I whispered.

"Come," she said as she offered her hand. She led me to her room through a corridor.

Her bedroom was gigantic. I peeked towards the ceiling. It was marvelously designed in wood with lighting all over the edges and in the centre. Her king-size bed was covered with a blue bedcover that had love quotes all over it. The walls were pink and the furnishings were pale blue. On the wall behind the bed, there was an eye-catching canvas of the sky with birds flying.

I made her sit on the bed as I pushed her down. She grinned. Removing her shirt, I threw it far away. She carved her hands inside my T-shirt and pulled it over my hands and then my neck, throwing it away on the floor.

"You are the most beautiful girl in the world, Shanaya; your skin is so soft and spotless," I complimented, holding her face with my hands, and planted a kiss on her cheeks.

In the next second, I hopped onto the bed and sat behind her. As slow as molasses syrup, I planted trailing kisses from her neck to the edge of the shoulder. My tongue whirled over her shoulder to her bra strap and my teeth bit her bare skin. She flinched.

"Your back is the sexiest thing in this world."

"Really?" she asked turning her face back.

'Yeah baby.'

Seconds later, I unclasped her bra with my teeth and it fell off. My hands quickly went to her breasts and cupped them.

"Slowly baby!"

She turned around, now her face was in front of mine, and I took her breast in my mouth.

"Ah!" She stifled a moan.

Her nipples were hard, which ran a stream of blood to my genitals, making my manhood erect at ninety degrees and I was sure she would be able to sense my erection on her leg.

She pushed me on the bed now and unbuttoned my jeans and in a quick motion, sliced it out through my legs. She came over me, grinning, and her teeth ground over my chest as her hand slipped into my boxer shorts. My back arched in anticipation.

"Ohh!!" I let out a sigh as she gripped my manhood with her cold fingers. My body trembled. I was on top of the world. She sat on my legs, glaring in my eyes unshakably, her tongue out in motion, seducing me even more and started fondling my chest with her left hand while her other hand was still inside my boxers, gently massaging my balls with her soft long fingers. She bestowed many feather-like kisses on my chest.

"Nikhil, I just love your chest. I want to lay on it forever."

Her fingers ran around the corner of my waist while gently peeling off my boxers with her gaze fixed on my face. For the first time in my life, I was naked in front of her. The muscles in my belly clenched, but in a dreamy pleasurable way, I wished this moment to never end.

Then I pushed her sidewards and again I was on top. I could not think straight and was caught in the moment.

"I think we should get you naked now, Shanaya."

"Umm!" She licked her lips.

Swiftly, I unbuttoned her denims and peeled it from her legs, as my tongue toured through every part of her legs.

"Anything you want, I am yours," she mumbled tilting her head, eyes closed.

I ran down my index finger from her foot to her pelvis making her body ache for my flesh. My tongue whirled repeatedly from her waist to her breast.

I shifted my body down and saw a wet spot on her baby pink panty which thrilled me more and I removed it slowly, admiring her beautiful, wet and pink vagina.

"Are you sure about this?" I asked catching my breath.

"Don't stop!! I want this," her voice was soft, yet authoritative.

"I don't have a condom," I confessed tugging her right nipple between my lips.

"Don't worry, I will take a pill."

I nodded.

I pushed her legs wide apart and my manhood poked her vagina.

I loomed over her, my body covering hers, rested my weight on my shoulders. She ran her hands on my naked back.

She was all wet down there. It was her first time. I gave a gentle thrust and she moaned. Her forehead dappled.

"Please, I want you inside me today, push harder," she begged.

"So impatient," I teased with a wide, salacious grin.

Her eyes flamed in desire, she stretched her arm and slapped my butt.

I thrust forward.

"Ohh my god!" she screamed out of pain, turning her face away, but patted my back, insinuating me to go on. Her head rocked against the pillow as I thrust again.

I looked down; there was some blood and her expressions hardened.

Ah! The first moan escaped from my lips as I thrust again and went deep inside her. My heart thumped like a train engine, holy shit! It was hot. She was smoking, skin-burning, goose bumps-inducing hot.

It was my first time too. I loved the feeling of being inside her. It was sizzling, wet and slippery; I have never felt like it before. I felt so close to her, it was too intimate. With my successive thrust, she started moaning in ecstasy and her hands were on my butt again.

"Harder please, bite my nipples, I beg you!" she screamed again taking a harsh breath, her arms around my back.

With each successive thrust, I could feel her getting wetter. I guided my hands in her long hair, playfully I pulled it.

"Nikhil?"

"Shanaya..."

"Look into my eyes and tell me that you will love me for life and beyond!"

Stopping myself for a moment, I looked into her eyes; the eyes I could die for.

"I will love you till my last breath."

Her lips curled into a smile and she pulled her head up to kiss me.

I paced myself, moving up and down over her body with my tongue on her nipples and then on her lips, moving just like a pendulum. She moaned again very loudly. "I am coming, please don't stop Nikhil," she growled out of pleasure, clasping her legs on my back.

"I love you too, baby, and I am close too."

She gripped my biceps snugly, feeling the heated muscles and then she put her hands around my back pulling me close, hugging her breasts.

With our bodies drenched in pleasure, we growled, moaned and then I felt the orgasm building up inside of me exploding.

"Nikhil!"

"Ahh," I moaned shooting my load inside her and fell over her, completely exhausted and satisfied. God! Why did it have to end, I wondered.

"I was curious, but didn't expect this to happen," Shanaya interjected my train of thoughts as she rested her head on my chest.

"I don't know what got into me today, when I saw you I just went on without thinking," I murmured as I covered both of our naked bodies with the blanket.

"Stop it! We love each other and we will get married soon, right?"

"Yes, very soon," I replied, kissing her on the forehead.

"Let's get dressed now. I will serve you lunch," she suggested.

"Sure, I am famished."

She got up from the bed covering her body with the blanket, bent down on the floor and picked up her clothes from the different parts of the room as she looked back at me, smiling.

"Can I have one more kiss?"

"Later, let me wear my clothes first," she replied and rushed towards the washroom. I got up from the bed and picked my boxers from the floor.

I kept the presents on her bed in her absence.

After a couple of minutes, she came out wearing her clothes again.

"Surprise!"

"Nikhil, I told you not to buy anything for me except the macaroons." She crossed her arms over her chest.

"Please, Shanaya, open it. I could not stop myself from buying stuff for you. I know you have to hide it from your mother, but please take them."

"For the last time, and from now on, no more gifts except on birthdays."

"Yes ma'am, please open them now."

She walked closer and sat beside me. One by one she tore the wrapping paper.

"These overcoats look amazing. Especially the blue one, look this will fit me perfectly."

She put it on.

"What do you think?"

"Awesome!" I yelled. "I am glad that you like it, what about the perfume?"

Shanaya opened the cap and brought the bottle near her nose. "Exquisite!"

It's the right moment to tell her about Blair, I thought.

"Shanaya, you know I made a new friend in Paris."

"Really?" she narrowed her eyes.

"Yes. I met her at the Queen Club. We had a couple of drinks together and then we danced."

"Nikhil, why didn't you tell me this before?" she asked, her cheeks flushed with anger.

"I thought you might feel bad as you told me not to do anything like that, but I was drunk that night."

"You guys danced, that's it, right?" She kept her hand on mine.

"We danced and then she asked me to go back to her place."

"What the fuck!" She pushed me away with her hands and stood up.

"Did you cheat on me?" she speculated, her eyes sparkled with tears. She was furious. Damn!

"Hell no!" I yelled defensively. "I love you, Shanaya, just listen to me first."

She took a deep breath.

"We were dancing and when she asked me out, I decided to put an end to it, and I did. That's all!"

"Okay, so you didn't ask for her number, and did you kiss her?" Her voice was loud and her fingers had now turned into a fist.

"Hell no, and yes, I took her number just to end that conversation with her politely."

"What for? Give me your phone!" She beckoned me with her fingers to pass the phone.

"I will delete her number right now and we can forget everything," she added.

"Shanaya, I am sorry for my behaviour," I apologized as I handed her my phone.

"Nikhil, I trust you. A little dancing is fine, but I don't want you to talk to her again. You are mine, only mine."

"Yes, I am all yours.'"

"Let's have lunch now," she said taking my hand in hers.

I was lucky that she didn't react that badly. God! It could have been a lot worse. I was so relieved taking that off my chest.

♋

Cruising back home, my mind repeatedly played snapshots of the incredible sex we just had. It was my first time too and it felt more beautiful than I thought it would. Perhaps because she was my soulmate. My face shone like the sun as I reminisced the most pleasurable moments of my life.

Later in the evening, on my bed, exhausted, I checked emails on my phone. My face quirked up when I found that there were more than twenty mails from the new clients I had made during my tour.

I sat up and started replying to them.

Around ten at night, my phone beeped. It was Shanaya.

"Hey."

"Shanaya, sorry, I almost forgot to call you."

"What are you up to?" she queried.

"I had a bunch of mails from new my clients. I had to sign and scan few contracts."

"Okay. I thought you might wanna talk about today. I can't stop myself from thinking about it."

"It was really great and incredible and I loved it. I am glad we did it." I smiled.

"Even I think the same way. It was so special."

"Did you take the pill?"

"Yes."

"Good night," she said before disconnecting the phone.

"Nikhil, why haven't you made the advances of these contracts yet?" Dad yelled and slapped the contracts on the table while I was checking the emails on my laptop, sitting in the office, scratching my head. He flopped onto the chair in front of me. I was taken aback as it was the first time he had reacted this way since we started working together.

Grasping the contracts from the table, I checked the details meticulously.

"Dad, there were some technical issues from the supplier's bank. I have notified their accounts team about the same, but the sales people are not coordinating properly due to which it got delayed," I defensively replied, but I was disheartened. Since the last two months, the day I returned from Paris, I had been burning the candle at both ends, but still, there was something or the other that was incomplete.

"Nikhil, make a conference call with the sales team and the bank and get this payment done. We are short of supplies," he suggested, leaning back in his chair, his face betraying his temper.

With my head tilted, I rolled my eyes contemplating his idea, which was good. I wondered why I hadn't come up with it. Experience speaks for itself, I guess.

"That sounds about right. I will do it immediately," I nodded.

As I saw the annoyance staggering away from his face, I started working again.

It was demotivating when things don't turn out well even though you have worked so hard, I thought, biting my lip. It had been a tradition to leave home early and work overnight every day.

All this while, Shanaya was furious. It had been two months since we last met.

Later in the evening, on my bed, I stretched myself. It had been a long, demanding day and all I wanted to do was lie down quietly.

Missing Shanaya, I started dialled her number.

"Hi. What's up?" I asked as I put my head on my arm.

"Hey you, nothing… bored all day. Exams are due next month."

"Can we meet tomorrow after my morning German class?"

"Don't you know it's Sunday? Mom never allows me to go out on weekends, Nikhil. You know that. It's been four years since we've been together!"

"Can't you make an excuse or something? You know on weekdays I come home around eight in the evening from office. Then it's too late for you."

"Mom won't let me go out because of exams. It's okay, you don't have to meet me."

"Please try."

"I can't meet you only at your convenience." Her voice came louder this time.

"It's not about whether it's convenient for me, you know how it is."

"I know, so stop it," she replied furiously.

And then she went on and on about how busy I was with my life and couldn't squeeze some time for her. It was really exhausting listening to her whine, as if I was having fun at the office. My eyes closed and I could not hear anything she said after a while. I did not respond for a couple of minutes.

"Nikhil, are you there? Did you fall asleep? Nikhil, wake up!"

Her voice startled me out of my stupor. Oh shit, how will I get out of this?

"No, no, I am listening to you. I am really sorry."

"Get lost!" She disconnected the phone as she shouted.

Apart from feeling sorry, I was irritated by her response. So what if I fell asleep for a moment? "I am exhausted," I said to myself.

♋

"Das ist sehr gut!" I heard my German teacher Shelly say while I was sitting quietly in my chair, with my hands on my cheeks. Though my mind was physically present in the class, it wandered around Shanaya's brown eyes.

I was missing her so much. Unable to control my feelings, I slid out the phone from my pocket. My eyes twinkled like stars the moment I saw Shanaya's picture on the wallpaper. While I was still furious about the way she reacted, but just like the previous times, my anger vanished again.

The moment the class ended, I stormed out and called Shanaya.

"Hi,"

"What do you want, Nikhil?" she said exasperatedly.

"I am sorry for yesterday."

"I am not a barking dog. How could you just fall asleep when I am talking to you?" I didn't know what to say.

"And you know that's not the worst part. I think from the day we had sex, you have lost interest in me," she accused acidly.

Every word stung my head like a bee sting. Knuckles clenched my fist too hard, involuntary my teeth gritted from the effort to calm myself and just not yell at her. My face boiled with anger.

She had crossed her limits this time. My love was tainted. I shook my head miserably. Why do girls have to bring sex as a weapon during fights? How could anyone lose interest in his girlfriend after having sex? I questioned myself. Can't she be more understanding during my difficult times? I just cannot take an off from work so that I can meet my girlfriend or maybe I could, but then again, she had to be patient and more empathetic.

"Shanaya, it's not at all like that. Trust me, I love you with all my heart, and don't just say something you don't mean," I replied swallowing my anger.

"No, I mean it. I just don't want to talk to you," she yelled and disconnected the phone.

What the hell! She did it again. I scooted towards my car and drove home.

Later in the evening, while watching a romantic love story on my laptop, my exasperation multiplied exponentially.

"Uff! Just another classic shitty love story with a happy ending: boy meets girl, they fall in love and later something happens and then they are finally together, happily ever after," I complained.

Movies should be made on things that happen after getting into a relationship with the ones you thought you can't live without. On how things get ugly and how in a middle of a day, all you want to do is to hang yourself or jump off a cliff to get relief from the suffocating relationship. Also, they should tell the world about how people are unwilling to compromise and the person who was once perfect according to them has the biggest number of flaws all of a sudden.

For the entire day, I was in a grouchy mood. Yet, the movie's happy ending somehow tranquilized my exasperation. At the end of the day, she was my girl, and I loved her so much. I decided to make up with her. I started typing.

Hi, can we meet tomorrow?

The phone beeped the moment I took the next breath.

Are you sure? Don't you have office tomorrow?

No, I will take the day off.

Suddenly, nostalgia hit me, reminding me of the good and happy times that I had spent with her.

Ok! Don't you dare cancel on me tomorrow as I have to tell my mother accordingly.

I will not dare to. It's been so long that I haven't seen my beautiful angel.

I am not mad at you Nikhil :). Let's meet at ten.

A smile turned up on my face. I realized that she was just irritated as I couldn't be there for her much these days. She wasn't wrong.

♋

It was exactly ten in the morning and I had reached the café. It had been a while since we had gone out on a date and I wanted it to be perfect to make her happy. For that, I had dressed my best today. Slamming my car's door, I ran inside the café.

My eyes spotted her sitting quietly on the chair, crossed legs, her hands on her cheeks, pondering. Her brown hair caught the morning sunlight and shone beautifully.

She was wearing a sport red T-shirt and blue-denim rugged shorts, looking irresistibly ravishing. I watched her like she had my heart in her fists and my soul on her feet.

She raised her head and saw me gazing at her. Her lips widened and cheeks turned crimson. She got up from the seat and walked towards me.

"Hi"

"Honestly speaking, you are looking like an angel, Shanaya," I complimented, gazing at her face as I ran down one finger over her cheek.

"Honestly?" She tilted her head with a mischievous smile on her face and in the next second she wrapped her arms around me.

"It's been a long time, Nikhil. I have missed you," she whispered as I felt her breath on my neck. "C'mon, I have ordered sandwiches and cold coffee for you."

"But I already have my hot coffee sitting beside me."

She blushed. I held her hand under the table and playfully glided it on her thigh, feeling her soft skin.

She constantly looked at me from under her dark curly eyelashes.

We talked, giggled and held hands as we ate. A small piece of cheese stacked to her upper lip.

I inched forward, my arms on her back now, my lips licked it away. She blushed looking around.

"I don't care, I love you, sweetheart."

As I was grabbing another bite of the delectable sandwich, I felt my phone's vibration in my pocket.

I took out my phone and typed the lock code. 'Pops' flashed on the screen.

I went out excusing myself and picked up the phone.

"Nikhil, you have to urgently come home. You skipped a few signatures on the contract that has to be mailed just right now."

"I am on the way, Dad," I said with a lump in my throat.

Even though I did not have a choice, I was scared to tell Shanaya that I had to leave early.

Sadly, I walked back to the table.

"Something important has come up and I have to go," I said softly.

"But it has been only an hour!" she said exasperatedly.

"I am really sorry. I will make up to you," I requested.

"Don't even try." Her eyes swelled up as she got up from the seat and walked away in a huff, without even looking back.

With my head down, I stood on the spot.

Holy crap! Nothing good had happened since the day I returned from Paris. Without any intention, I always seemed to hurt her in some way or the other. I called her repeatedly to apologize, but she rejected my call every single time.

♋

At twilight, when I was about to leave from office, I heard my phone ringing. It was Shanaya.

"I am really sorry for today," she said.

"It's okay." I sighed in relief.

"I will be going to celebrate Nikita di's birthday party tonight," I told her to ease my awkwardness.

"But her birthday is tomorrow, right?" she asked confused.

"Yeah, but she wants to celebrate tonight."

"Can you call me at midnight? I will wish her then," she requested.

"Sure. And I will make up to you."

"I will wait for it then."

"I love you," I said as I desperately wanted her to say it back.

She didn't reply and hung up.

Later in the club, I was standing by the bar, the loud ear-splitting music being my only friend there, as I watched my sister and her friends, dancing passionately. Suddenly I saw Radhika, my old school friend approaching me. I was not sure whether to talk or just ignore her as I hadn't spoken to her for a while. I took another sip of my drink when Radhika finally walked up to me.

"Hey, Nikhil, how have you been? Long time no see."

"Hi Radhika, it's really great to see you after such a long time," I said smiling.

"What are you doing these days?" she asked.

"I have joined my family business," I simpered.

"Oh! But you always talked about studying in Germany."

"Yes, I did. Nonetheless, I settled here, my family wants me to be around," I replied. "What about you?" I enquired.

"I am working with an e-commerce company."

"Oh, that's a quite an emerging market these days," I said tilting my head.

"You are absolutely right."

We chit chatted for another five minutes. She pryingly enquired about Shanaya and my relationship with her.

She was as usual too curious about us.

"I have come here with our school mates, wanna come and say hi?"

"Sure."

After meeting my old friends, nostalgia hit me. Walking back to the table, I checked my wrist watch, it was almost twelve.

I waved to my sister from the distance onto the dance floor and signalled her to come to cut the cake. All of her friends gathered around the table quickly.

One of my sister's friends opened the cake box and kept it on the round table. I lit the candles.

Nikita bent down and blew out the candles. Everybody sang happy birthday in chorus, while clapping along.

Shortly after eating the cake, I took out my phone from my pocket. My jaw dropped.

There were five missed calls from Shanaya.

"Fuck! I am screwed big time," I bellowed. I ran outside the club and dialled her number nervously this time.

"I am sorry, Shanaya. I didn't hear your call, the music was very loud."

"Stop it already, Nikhil. You lie... lied to me," she babbled.

What now? I cried in my mouth.

"I lied about what, Shanaya?" I asked, completely clueless.

"That you are with your sister. I know you are with Radhika," she accused me as her voice fumbled.

I looked around with my lips sealed. How the hell did she come to know that I had met Radhika? God! This was awkward, how will you get out of this one Nikhil?

"Shanaya, yes, I crossed paths with her tonight, but I am with my sister."

"Don't you dare lie to me again. I just saw a check-in where she tagged you on Facebook."

"I don't want to argue; I will just give my phone to my sister,"

Her voice was louder, trembling now, she was crying horribly.

"Tell me honestly. Nikhil, are you with her or not?" she asked calming herself as I heard her taking a deep breath.

"It's my sister's birthday, dammit! Can you talk sense for a change?" I yelled. My head was about to burst.

"Forgive me for overreacting, but we have been fighting a lot these days. I was taken over by a dark cloud of jealousy. I love you."

"I don't want to talk to you now. You don't trust me at all. I am not sure how we will survive this relationship if we can't even trust each other. Good night." I disconnected the phone.

She should have trusted me. This time she had really crossed a line and I was determined that I would not talk to her for a few days. I had never imagined that after four years of a perfect relationship, I would face such complications.

Back in the club, I saw everybody was having dinner as it was about to shut down. I sat down quietly, served myself and began eating. Her words constantly rattled around my head, fuelling my temper. How could she even imagine that I would lie to her like that? In our four years together, I had never lied to her about anything. And my honesty was one of the things she loved about me, I pondered scratching my beard.

♋

On my way back home, my phone repeatedly beeped. As I was driving, I took out the phone from my pocket and saw Shanaya's name on the home screen. Irritably shaking my head, I put down my phone.

"What happened Nikhil?" Nikita asked turning her face towards me.

"Everything is fine, just feeling sleepy," I lied through my teeth and continued driving.

It seemed that these days I had been the culprit for everything. Five minutes with Radhika would now cost me a week full of fights.

I was so furious at her; I chose not to talk to her for a week this time.

While on my bed, lost in my fickle thoughts, I called Varun. I desperately needed a friendly ear.

"Hi Varun, how are you?"

"Look who's calling. Is it raining outside?" he asked humorously.

"Oh, shut up! Don't be so dramatic."

"Ha-Ha, anyway, how are you? How's Shanaya?"

"Yeah, everything is fine," I tried to say casually.

"Tell me honestly, what happened, you sound very low today."

"Nothing as such man, we have been fighting a lot recently."

"Why?"

"I have been pretty occupied with my work lately and haven't been able to take out time for her."

"Then take out time for her, she is your girl, man."

"I can only meet her on weekends but her mother doesn't allow her to go out then."

"Take an off from work then."

"I can't take off every week to meet her, you know."

"Get married then, I will talk to uncle, ha-ha." He hooted.

"Yeah sure, right. Hear me out first."

He listened very patiently to everything as he had always been a good listener. I also told him about what had happened. Empathizing with my situation, he suggested, "First of all, always listen to her patiently and try to understand whatever she wants to say. The most effective way to make a girl happy is to hear her out in detail. Make her feel that whatever she is saying is very important to you." He paused.

"Always try to work things out otherwise your relationship will die. Try to keep jealousy out of the room. If something is bothering Shanaya, resolve the issue, don't let it remain hanging."

"I do try that, but sometimes it gets out of hand," I replied.

"Nikhil, you love her, right?"

"So much that your words feel so unspeakably lame."

"Then try to spend some more time with her from now on."

"I think you are right," I said, convinced.

I was about to hang up when I heard the beep sound of a call waiting. I brought my phone closer to my face and saw that it was Shanaya.

I just wanted to ignore her calls, but after talking to Varun, my mind had changed.

"Hey, Varun, wait... will call you back."

I picked up Shanaya's call.

"Shanaya," I said.

"Nikhil, who were you talking to this late at night?" she almost yelled.

"I was talking to Varun. Stop yelling!"

"Varun, Ha-Ha, good one," she replied with a sarcastic laugh.

"What is that supposed to mean?" I asked. I was on the edge, but as Varun had suggested, I tried to stay calm and took a deep breath.

"Varun or Radhika?" she queried, heatedly this time.

Her name evaporated my wits. My eyebrows squeezed together to form a crease and my nostrils flared. My fingers rolled into a fist and I punched the air.

"Shanaya, why all of a sudden are you bringing Radhika into this?"

"Since you are not interested in me anymore, you must be thinking of giving her a chance. After all, she loved you for such a long time."

That did it. I screamed at her.

"I have to wake up early and go to work. I don't want to take your shit anymore."

Agitated, I disconnected the call and lay on my stomach on my bed. I just wanted to relax and not think about her for a very long time now.

Never in these four years had I felt so stressed in my relationship. It was always full of hearts, sweet talk, smiles and feather-like kisses, but this time it was going out of control. I was out of control; never in my life was I this annoyed and frustrated. Her lack of faith kicked me in the crotch this time and the pain was unbearable.

That night I almost wet my bed because of nightmares. One included Shanaya shooting me with a gun. And then there was another in which Shanaya was cheating on me with her college professor. Damn! Both of the nightmares bent my soul and scared me to death.

♋

"My life is a mess," I mumbled sitting on my bed closing my eyes and tilting my head back. My mind was a railway track today, with endless thoughts running over it like a train. Two months had passed and still Shanaya and I fought every day like two ferocious bears. Our fights increased as the day passed by, sometimes turning so ugly that we ended up abusing each other.

The morning messages which once used to bring a smile on my face were enough to extract joy for a week, as they were always about something that I did wrong the previous night. Late night talks, which rejuvenated my body earlier after a hectic day, helped me getting panic attacks for breakfast. And there were nights when she didn't even call before sleeping and when I did, her phone was always busy. She was no longer concerned about where I was going or to whom I was talking to whenever my phone was busy. Jealousy was like a divorced wife now.

Words like 'I love you' and 'I miss you' became redundant and obsolete forms of expressing love now. She always had a very long list of good things which I apparently never did now, but allegedly used to when we had fallen in love.

Vulnerable, I saw my relationship being flushed down the toilet. Apart from all this crap, I still loved her and hoped that one day we'd be together and stronger in love.

Hoping for a brighter sun, I texted her to meet me.

After a couple of minutes, my phone buzzed. She had replied: *Okay*

♋

With my palms resting on my face at the restaurant the next day, I was hoping to clear things with Shanaya. I had been waiting for an hour, and wondered whether she was coming or not.

I gulped the fourth glass of water. I had no choice but to wait. She was the love of my life and I couldn't afford to lose her. I was completely lost in my thoughts when I saw her approaching towards me, walking as slowly as she could. I jumped from my seat and extended my arms to hug her.

She rolled her eyes and looked away while she sat down on the couch, completely ignoring my gesture.

I gazed at her, but she constantly looked away. I decided to break the ice, inched closer and swallowed.

"Shanaya, please let's try to work things out here. We have been fighting a lot lately. But I want to spend my entire life with you."

"Please! Don't talk forever and shit, Nikhil. I don't think you love me at all now." She gave me a dirty look and crossed her legs.

"I will always love you, Shanaya. You are my first and last love," I said staring at her.

"I want to drink something today, let's order vodka with sprite," she demanded, turning her face away.

"As you wish."

Waving towards the waiter, I placed the order. She was as silent as the stars. I took her hand and said, "Shanaya, I want this relationship to last for life and beyond, and I am sure you want it too. Tell me, how can we forget everything and just start again with a clean slate?"

"I don't know Nikhil. You have changed a lot." She shrugged.

"I haven't changed at all, Shanaya. I am your same pumpkin, and it's just that we have been quarrelling a lot lately."

"No, you have, Nikhil!" She gave a dismissive wave of her hand. "You don't even listen to me now. You don't like to meet or talk. Do you remember the time when we used to chat constantly for hours when our relationship began? Where is that spark?"

I inclined towards her and said, "The spark is still there, let me show you."

While closing my eyes, I brought my face close to her lips. In the next second, I felt an impulsive force on my chest, pushing me away. My eyes flew open.

She glared at me and rose from her seat.

It was very weird and unexpected. She raised a hand and yelled, "Don't you dare touch me, Nikhil! Are we in this relationship so that we can be physical? I must tell you that I am not that kind of a girl."

I was aghast and tongue-tied. I glanced around the restaurant, luckily it was empty. Lord! I would have been embarrassed. This was the first time when she literally pushed me away and said something like that. The push felt like she had literally thrown me away from her heart and from her life.

"I am sorry, please sit down, and I will not touch you again," I pleaded with my palms together as my eyes welled up. Tears flooded from inside of me and so did my self-esteem.

"Fine," she replied, sitting down. The waiter bought a couple of vodka shots and kept in front of her on the table. The very next moment, she grabbed the shot and then gulped it like water followed by the other one.

"Slow down, Shanaya, there is no rush."

"Tell me, Nikhil, what is it that you want me to forget and start again?" she said, her voice getting louder this time.

"Why are you talking like this?"

"You want me to forget that you have completely lost interest in me or that you don't have the balls to tell your dad that you want to meet your girlfriend?"

Her malicious words shattered me to bits.

"Shanaya, why are you being so rude to me today?" I wiped my tears.

"I am not rude at all. I think you might be talking to Radhika as you don't call me at night anymore." She folded her arms.

"Why do you always have to bring a gun to a knife fight? From where did Radhika jump into this? Whenever I call, either you are sleepy or you want to talk to your friends."

"Really? I always waited for hours to talk to you before sleeping. I am tired of doing it now. Am I wrong if I am thinking about my sleep this time for a change?"

I had never felt so low about myself in my entire life. She made me feel like a selfish person and a loser too.

"It's always been about you – Nikhil, your friends, your family, and your mood. Did you ever think about me? Answer honestly," she went on and on as she gazed at me.

The river full of insult and humiliation soaked me to the skin. I decided that I couldn't take it anymore.

"Shanaya, I am going to Mumbai tomorrow for a couple of days to attend a conference, take your time and call me if you want to be with me. I can't take it anymore," I said as I got up from the couch and left without looking at her.

♋

The two days straight in the conference, I checked my phone more than a hundred times, but she didn't text or call even once. On the other hand, I didn't initiate as her heart-ripping words were still rattling inside my head. The conference in Mumbai went well as I was able to meet new clients and could settle pending claims from the existing clients. As the conference was successful, I decided to forget everything she had said and start afresh.

The message was sent by an old friend.

Hi Nikhil, it took me a lot of courage to finally tell you that Shanaya and I have been talking for the past couple of months. Earlier, when we started talking, she didn't tell me that she is in a relationship with you. After many days, when I finally proposed to her, she confessed that she likes me too, but she was with you then. I know you both have been in a lot of fights these days, but whatever or whosoever she chooses to spend her life with should be aware of what actually is happening here, so I thought to let you know about this. I couldn't bear the guilt of sneaking behind your back to meet and talk to her. I just wanted to clear the air, so that we are on the same page.

Unnervingly, I grabbed the corner of my bed in a desperate attempt to stabilize myself. I sat down. I was not able to believe whether this is actually happening. Was I in the middle of a nightmare? I gawked towards Varun repeatedly and shook my head just to confirm that this was the reality. My heart was beating outside my chest and I felt it aching for the first time in my life. It felt like a heart attack.

"Nikhil, are you okay? Say something," Varun loomed closer, unable to sit still, his black eyes brimming with concern.

I took a harsh breath. Tears squirted from my eyes.

My body was bloodless. I felt desiccated, words failed me. I could not move my legs.

"Nikhil, you are not blinking your eyes!" he shouted and put his arms around me. His eyes welled up as he shook me.

Not possible! It can't be true! My subconscious was figuratively screaming at me.

"Varun, I am telling you; it can't be true. Shanaya loved me so much. She just can't cheat on me like that," I said defending my love.

"It can't be true, it can't be true," I shook my head repeatedly, calming myself.

"Why don't you call Shanaya and confirm? Maybe it's not true, even I am not sure about it," Varun suggested as he sat back on the bed.

My mind was baffled. I took a quick look towards Varun. "I will call her right now," my voice wobbled.

I got up and scurried to the balcony. My hands shivered as I dialled her number on the screen pad.

I could feel my heart beating on my neck.

"Shanaya," I cried.

"Hi Nikhil, are you fine?" she asked sceptically.

"You know, Varun just told me that you are having an affair with somebody else and you are double timing with me. I want you to tell me the truth," I said, getting straight to the point.

"What?" she roared.

"Who told him that? He is lying. I love you, baby."

"Shanaya, tell me the truth!"

"If you don't trust me anymore, then I don't want to talk to you." She disconnected the phone immediately.

"What the heck!" I yelled.

My blood flamed, anger spread in every part of my body. Furious, I dialled her number again, but she disconnected it immediately.

My phone beeped. She texted. *With mom, can't talk.*

I shoved the phone in my pocket and went inside the room when I heard Varun's mobile ringing.

"Why is she calling me?" Varun came closer, his eyebrow lifted and extended his hand to show me his phone.

My eyes narrowed and lips tightened.

"Pickup... Maybe... she doesn't know that you are with me, and put it on speaker," I stammered as my suspicion was turning into truth as she had just texted that she was with her mom. But now she had called him.

"Varun, why the hell are you spreading rumours about me? Who told you that I was having an affair with somebody else?" Her voice was loud.

"Shanaya, Raj told me that you guys are dating. He even sent me screenshots of your messages," he answered calmly.

"He is faking it. I will just call him and give him a piece of my mind." She hung up.

My legs shook like a leaf and I fell down on the floor after listening to her. Instead of talking to me, she said she would talk to Raj and scold him; she did cheat on me. Her words were a shotgun to my heart and it scattered into invisible infinite atoms. My fingers curled into a fist and with a swift motion, I smashed my fist on the floor. My hands went numb as thick red blood appeared on my fingers.

"What are you doing, Nikhil?" Varun yelled shrinking back. He froze and stared with wide eyes. He got up and pulled out a white handkerchief and wrapped it around my fingers to stop the blood.

Suddenly, adrenaline spiked through my body. I got up and called Shanaya again.

I waited for a couple of rings with my phone pressed to my ear. This time she answered.

"Shanaya, Varun is with me right now and I heard everything. I know that this is tr... true..." My tongue slipped as my chest vibrated. "But I just need one single answer from you and then you will never hear my voice again. Why did you cheat on me?" I jumped down her throat, my voice louder than ever.

She started howling.

"I... I am sorry, Nikhil," she stammered. With the phone pressed on my cheek, I fell down breathless.

I was not expecting this answer from her, at least so soon. God! Some part of me wanted to give her the benefit of doubt, but she eradicated all the bewilderment in a second. I cringed, my stomach groveled and it felt like the most painful experience of my life.

Her words entered my bloodstream rapidly and I thought my veins might burst. My head started spinning and every fiber of my body yelled why! Why god, why me!

"Shanaya, you have no idea what you have lost. One day you will realize that my love for you was pure. I did everything I could in this relationship and since you still cheated on me, you will never be satisfied in your entire life. I can't believe that you have been lying through your teeth all this while." My shoulders sagged, sadness spread all over my face.

"Don't say that Nikhil, I only love you, don't leave me. I made a mistake, please forgive me!"

"Shanaya, you just stained my love for life. This thing will haunt me till my death bed. I can never forget what you did to me," I cried shaking with sobs.

"Nikhil, please forgive me. I will never do this again. It was a bad phase of my life. We were fighting constantly and you did not have time for me. It was a weak phase and his friendship comforted me. I was lonely," she mourned.

"Stop it! Enough! You were lonely and you started lying and cheating. In just the span of a couple of months, you drifted away from me. Now it all makes sense,'

I swallowed hard. "I will still pray that you get whatever you wish in your life. And one more important thing, please, never cheat on Raj. It is the worst pain someone can give in this world. You have given that to me, so I can tell, but still, it was worth it. I had the love of my life for four years. After all, love is about giving everything to that one special person. I have no regrets here," I said while wiping my tears.

"Please stop, Nikhil. I am sorry. I did a horrible thing and I know I don't deserve your forgiveness, but still, I beg you to give me one more chance. I got diverted, my mind just played a trick on me..." she squealed.

"Shanaya, I may forgive you with time, but I can't give you another chance. You taught me a lesson today, never trust anyone in this world or else you will be hammered into pieces. Your life will be miserable." My hands covered my forehead as I tapped my feet unconsciously.

"Goodnight Shanaya, it was nice knowing you. Bye." I loosened the first couple of buttons of my shirt. The heat seemed stifling.

"Don't hang up, please I beg you, please, I am sorry."

Her constant apologising really made my hackles rise! Anger stormed upon me. I felt like bursting like a volcano. I stood up.

"You are not sorry. Shanaya, you just never anticipated that your little secret will come out like this!" I bellowed. "What's the point of saying sorry, Shanaya? You did what you wanted. You broke my heart; you've ruined me."

"I can't let you go. No one has ever loved me the way you did. Please forgive me. Please, I beg you. I can't hate myself more than

I do right now. Forgive me. I will die without you. What is left for me in this life, if not you?" she asked agitatedly.

"You should have thought before jeopardizing our relationship, there is no point crying about it now. Anyway, have a great future ahead. Bye," I said and disconnected my phone.

I threw my phone on my bed and fell on the floor again, but harder this time. Tears were constantly coming out of my eyes.

"Nikhil, I am sorry. It's better that you got to know about this now. Imagine what would have happened if you'd have come to know about this after marrying her," Varun consoled me.

"Sh… She should not have done this to me," I stammered.

"Nikhil, you are my best friend. I am always with you. Please don't react like this. Things will get better."

"What will be better? More swords in my stomach or maybe on my back," I said sarcastically, a headache coming on.

"You will forget her with time."

"Argh! I don't want to forget her," I protested and continued. "I can never stop loving her. She was the one for me. In these past four years, I never thought of any other girl, not even in my dreams. I was so committed to her. I can't think of cheating on her ever."

"I understand."

"Varun, did Raj tell you how it all started?" I snorted.

"In fact, he did. He said that it all started through Facebook, and then they started exchanging messages, eventually talking on the phone. They also met a couple of times when she lied to you that she was going to meet her cousin in the hospital. They both began to like each other and Shanaya was confused about whom to choose between you and him, so he decided to inform you so that at least you guys would break up."

A tremor ran down my vertebrae, as his words pierced my ears. Suddenly I felt a pump in my biceps muscles. I just wanted to punch Raj on his face.

"I feel like killing that bastard now, but there is no point of blaming the race track if you have a broken engine," I muttered.

"Let's go out. I don't want my family to know about this; they will be worried."

"Okay," he nodded.

We walked to the door when suddenly someone grabbed my hand from behind.

It was Nikita.

"I want to go with you," she requested, her voice soft.

"I am just coming back in ten minutes."

"Please take me with you," she pleaded.

"Leave me alone. I don't want to talk to anyone right now," I yelled.

She raised her head, looked into my eyes and lay her arms around me.

"I know, Nikhil."

My eyes narrowed to crinkled slits, lips quivered, wondering how the hell she knew about it. For one tiny second, I thought that maybe she was referring to something else. But a tear drifted away from her eye. She stared impatiently into my eyes wanting me to say yes.

Immediately I wrapped her around my arms, my body trembling with sobs.

"Let's go! Dad will see you crying. He saw you very happy after a very long time today. I don't want to take that happiness away from him," Nikita suggested.

"Are you sure you want to drive?" Nikita asked the moment I sat on the driver's seat.

"Hmm. Yes." I nodded.

Pressing the accelerator hard, I drove the car towards a secluded place nearby. My hands were hardly able to steer the wheel. Minutes later, I stopped and immediately got out of the car, and so did Nikita and Varun.

I gazed towards the sky intensely and dropped down to my knees.

"Why god, why me! I loved her so much. I prayed to you for her," I cried with my hands folded in front of my chest.

Nikita crawled closer and put her comforting arms around me.

"Get up," she requested.

I felt like a tree uprooted by the storm. As if god was taking revenge for having a perfect life before. First, my mother suffered from a life-threatening disease, secondly, I worked my ass off to bring my business into profit and now the slap of the ultimate betrayal.

It was just too painful to digest. Moreover, I was innocent in all the three situations. I mean, it was not because of my deeds. But I guess life always has more to offer.

Suddenly, the wind blew as cold as ice and I looked around. The wind thrashed the branches of the trees followed by lightning and thundering. Apparently, nature was taking revenge for my agony and was preparing a comfortable bed for the night. My veins throbbed in my neck.

"Sis, for the first time in months, I was making progress in my life. I had been as happy as a lark because of the success in the conference. But it seems I am not allowed to be happy anymore," I said miserably.

"Don't say that. Nikhil, I am always with you. We will get out of this," she replied.

"Thanks for saying we…" I mumbled.

"Sis, tell me one thing. How can things change from here? I cannot run back in time. I just can't understand one thing. Why did she do it? Was I not good enough of her? Was my love fake? Is Raj a better man? If that's the thing then, she should have just told me and I would have broken up with her at once," I whined with my hands on my stomach.

"She is a fool, she doesn't know that she kicked away a man who loved her day and night. I bet no one can love her more than you did," she said sympathetically.

"Nikhil, it's all her loss. See the bright side here, you learned a lesson and you will never trust anybody again blindly," Varun interrupted.

"I can just see dark, gloomy clouds in front of me. God, if my love was not true, then I should be dead at this very instant!" I let out a scream.

"Bro, she was not worthy of your love. Soon you will have someone better in your life," Varun said, sensitively.

I frowned and said turning my head towards him. "I can never trust anyone in my life now, and especially girls. I am done with girls."

In life, I could survive financial instability, medical illness or any other calamity, but betrayal was intolerable and that too when you had been honest throughout. My subconscious recollected her lies when she said she was going out to meet her friends; maybe she had met him at that time and lied to me about it. I was going crazy with the random thoughts. I was so furious at her, I wanted to skin her alive, but then my subconscious whispered to me saying that the damage was already done, there was no point of punishing her.

"Let's go back home, our parents will worry," my sister suggested.

I nodded.

After dropping Varun, I went straight to my room. It had been a long day for me and with this soul-thrashing face of reality, I just wanted to lie down on my bed alone. When I checked my phone, I saw more than a hundred missed calls from Shanaya. What did she want now?

Damn! I felt as as stupid as an ass. I had always trusted her, never doubted a single thing she ever said. Maybe that was my fault. A little possessiveness might have saved my relationship, but I always thought that love can never fade and if someone has to cheat, then one will, even after being overprotective. On the contrary, she was always possessive of me. She consistently checked my phone whenever we met, always enquired on every occasion my phone was busy, asking who I was talking to, and if I was talking to a female friend then why at night, and then suggesting me to talk to them in the day time, etc., etc. I tried everything so that she remained happy and satisfied in this relationship. But I failed.

Life can be cruel sometimes; one moment you are happy and thankful for whatever you have and the very next moment it changes everything. I, today, was thanking god for my success in the conference and for Shanaya and my family, and in a split of a second, I lost the love of my life. I was drowning in the sea of sadness.

"Nikhil, get up and have your dinner. You must be starving," my sister ordered bringing me my dinner.

"I can't gulp down a single thing right now. I will vomit. Please don't force me. I will eat in the morning," I begged.

"Please, for me, just a few bites," she requested.

"I can't, sis. I just can't," I said as I covered my face with the blanket.

She sat next to me and held my hand.

"Everything will be fine eventually."

I kept my silence and she tried her best to console me.

"When and how did you come to know about this, sis?" I asked in desperation.

"Varun called me when you were not picking his calls as you were in the conference. He asked me about you and then he told me everything. I was so overwhelmed in agony when I came to know about it, but I did not have the courage to tell you. I am so sorry, Nikhil," she said as she started weeping.

"I don't know what to say, I am torn to shreds," I said.

"I am here with you. We will survive this, just have faith in god." She leaned back and looked up.

I was so hurt, I didn't get a wink of sleep. The February moon filtered through the brown windows of my room, played on the marble flooring trying to eliminate the darkness in my head, but that was just not enough. I repeatedly questioned myself, why me? How can I ever come out of this dreadful situation? I can't love any other girl. My stomach muscles clenched in severe pain. I think betrayal is the most brutal way of hurting someone. In movies, people often try to take revenge, but I couldn't hurt her, I didn't want to give her any kind of pain. I will try to forgive her eventually!

"Nikhil, get up son!" I heard my dad shout.

"Coming, Dad," I screamed back.

I slowly opened my bleary eyes. I stretched and yawned on my bed. Blinking a few times, I gave a couple of moments for my pupils, soaked in agony, to become comfortable.

"Finally, it's morning," I sighed. Last I checked, it was four in the morning and I was broken and exhausted. I had no clue when I finally fell asleep.

In the bathroom, I stood staring at myself in the big mirror, looking like a ghost with my eyes swollen and face all pale. Even a child could tell that I had been crying all night. The painful memory of the betrayal hit me again with a sledged hammer. My face muscles tightened up and a tear trekked down my cheek. I could not look at myself.

I was not prepared to tell my parents about the break-up, so I thought I'd appear as bright as I could. Within seconds, I washed my face and walked towards my dad's room.

Mom and Dad were having their morning tea on the chairs near the coffee table.

"Good morning, son," Dad darted an interested eye at me as he took another sip of his tea.

"Good morning Dad… Mom," I murmured.

I sat on the bed, folding my legs.

"It's 10 a.m. You got up so late today. Tired because of the conference?" Mom murmured.

The soul breaking betrayal I came to know of might leave me tired for the rest of my life. Act normally, Nikhil! I mumbled to myself.

"Well, my stomach hurts a bit. Maybe something I ate in Mumbai yesterday," I lied. I had no intention to go to work.

"You can rest today. You have done a great job yesterday. I am so happy because of you." Dad leaned back in his chair, arms rested on his lap.

"Thanks, Dad." If only they knew what I had got in return for doing the great work at the conference.

"Some tea?" My mom insisted with her chin up.

"Sure."

"Where is Nikita?" I raised an eyebrow.

"She left for office early. I don't know why, but she seemed upset," Mom pouted, her hands rested on her sides.

"I am afraid I have no clue, Mom," I lied while taking the teacup from mom.

What could I have possibly said at that moment, I wondered taking a tentative sip.

Suddenly, Shanaya's words 'I am sorry! I am sorry!' rang in my depressed and tormented head. My body felt weak. I was tongue-tied and my hands felt motionless. Something surged from my gut into my mouth. My mouth twisted. I almost vomited the bare amount of tea I had swallowed a couple of seconds before.

I looked up and saw mom looking tense.

"Nikhil, have some medicine. It seems severe."

"Okay, Mom," I murmured, turning my face away from her.

"Nikhil, are you fine, son? Is anything bothering you?" Dad asked with concern as he got up from his chair and sat beside me.

"No no, nothing at all, Dad," I stammered.

"Fine, go rest now. Just let me know the settlement with the suppliers," he requested.

"Okay." I nodded.

I trailed back to my room and lay down on my bed. I recalled old memories from the past when I was with her. The time when we smiled holding hands, to the day when I heard the whisper of her heart telling me that she loved me as I rested my head on her chest. And then the day when she kissed me for the first time and my head quaked with ecstasy. I remembered every time when we met and her face glowed like the faithful sun. I was in a quandary whether her body was faking her love too, or maybe the way she used to care for me whenever I was under the weather, or the time when she kept a fast so that I get a decent score in GRE, or the time she prayed with her hands folded in the temple for my mother's health… could all these things possibly be fake?

Happiness goes away very quickly, I guess. I cried my eyes out, hiding my face under the blanket.

♋

Next morning, I opened my eyes and quickly squinted towards the wall clock and it said ten.

"Oh god, late again!" I wondered why Shanaya didn't wake me up as she used to wake me up every morning. I ran through the logs and messages when an overwhelming sorrow knotting my stomach struck me. I recalled the agonizing truth of my life. We were no longer together!

I missed Shanaya, my eyes welled up. I wanted to meet her and hold her in my arms. I got up from the bed and started getting ready for office.

After my bath, as I was combing my hair, I heard my phone ringing in the bedroom.

"Who might it be at this time?" I said, paused and then continued combing.

Running towards the phone lying on my bed, I saw an unknown number flashing on the screen.

I shrugged and swiped my thumb to the right.

"Hello."

"Boo hoo, forgi... me..." A lamenting cacophony barged out from my phone's speaker.

It turned out to be a girl's voice crying endlessly. I could not figure out who it was, but some part of me said that it was Shanaya.

Although I was furious at her, the thought of her crying like that shook me and without more ado, I said "Shanaya, is that you?"

"Nikhil, I am sorry," she said clearing her throat.

"I don't want to talk to you," I bellowed.

"Nikhil, please don't hang up. I am standing outside your home, please meet me for the last time."

"What's the point of meeting now?" I demanded.

"I want to talk to you, please come," she coaxed.

"Well, okay. I will come down."

The truth was: I wanted to meet her too. I had missed her in the last few days. I just wanted to check how she was doing. My body ached to hug her. After all, I was the innocent one. I took my car keys and went downstairs. She was standing near the main door.

"Let's go somewhere else. Sit in the car," I ordered looking at her face for a brief second. The sun was shining hard and I felt the sweat on my back.

I didn't want anyone at home to know about this. Within seconds, I drove the car to a nearby place and parked it.

I glanced towards her. In the blaze of afternoon light, her grave face made my body shiver.

She looked like she hadn't eaten in the last two days, her eyes swollen and under eye circles were deep and dark. She was devastated and constantly crying while staring down at her knuckles. At that moment, I just wanted to hold her tightly in my arms and tell her that everything would be fine, even though she had broken my heart. I could not see her in that miserable state.

"Shanaya, why are you crying like that?" I turned sideward towards her.

She squared her shoulders, her head held high.

"Nikhil, I beg you, please forgive me. I committed a heinous crime and I am very sorry about it. Please don't take your love away from me. I will die without you."

Her words made me shed tears from inside. I was not able to see her in that wretched state, but the truth was that I couldn't trust her again.

"I am sorry, but I cannot be in a relationship with anyone now. You have broken my trust, I am ruined," I blurted, my lips closed and I glanced away from her.

"Don't say that! I will die without you." She burst into more tears. She rubbed her hands on her thighs.

"Shanaya, why don't you move on with Raj? Don't you like him anymore?" I suggested although my heart knew that god would punish me for saying all this.

"No! No!" she shrieked as she shook her head again and punched her fist into the dashboard.

"Shanaya, stop it!" My eyes widened and my mouth fell open. I grabbed her wrist.

"Nikhil, I never liked him. He intruded into our relationship at a weak point and I could not stop him. I was not in my senses. I just love you. Everybody makes a mistake. Mine is the biggest, I know, please forgive me. Life is so big. How will I live every second without you? Please think about it and try to forgive me."

She cried harder, squirming in her seat.

Every time I looked at her, she rolled her eyes and stared outside the car. I could feel her body trembling.

"Please forgive me; I beg you, give me another chance." She folded her hands together in front of me.

"Shanaya, you are a nice girl, please don't plead. I don't like it. It's not that I don't want to forgive you, but I just can't. Maybe with time I will," I said putting my hands on the steering wheel.

"I will wait for you. Even if you don't come back in five years, I will still wait. I will seek forgiveness from god and I am sure as my love for you is true, you will eventually come back." Tears raced down her cheeks.

I turned my face and grabbed the water bottle from the backseat, extending my hand.

"Here, drink some water!"

"I don't want to." She rubbed her eyes.

I widened my eyes and gave her an unnerving stare.

"Okay, sorry, give it to me," she said.

I handed her the bottle and she opened the cap and gulped a couple of sips.

"Please, Nikhil, please give me something so that I can remember you and live my life alone, even if you decide that your happiness doesn't belong with me." She tucked her hair behind her ear.

"I have nothing to give, I am helpless."

"Can you promise that if I prove my love, then you will forgive me?"

I was sure that I would never get back with her, but my heart fought with my brain hazardously and forced me to give her that promise. She should have some kind of hope in her life to survive, my subconscious told me.

"Okay, if you prove your love in a couple of years, then I will forgive you and take you back."

"Can you please say that again? I will record it on my phone and will listen to it again and again?"

"Okay."

Her tears melted me; during the entire time we were together, I could not abide her tears. She took out her phone from her beige coloured bag and pressed the recording button.

"Shanaya, I promise that if you prove your love in a couple of years then I will give you another chance."

"Thank you very much, Nikhil. This means a lot to me. I will listen to it every second and will wait for you forever." Her face turned into a smile. She slouched onto the seat and crossed her legs.

I inched closer to her and put my hands on her face. Gently extending my thumbs, I wiped her tears. Damn, I so wanted to hug her right away.

If it was actually possible, I would have taken her pain away in a second. God knew that I had loved her for a very long time; those feelings aren't going away in a day or two. I wanted to tell her that I still love her, but I restrained myself.

"Shanaya, you are a nice girl, everything will be fine. Just don't cry now."

"Nikhil, can I hug you for once, please?"

I didn't know how to respond to it, so I kept mum, but she insisted again, "Please, for me."

"Okay," I replied scratching my beard.

In a flash, she put her hands around me and held me as snugly as possible and started crying again.

"I am sorry, I hurt the most beautiful thing that happened to me in my entire life. Please god, forgive me. I can do anything for you, Nikhil. You just say it, even if you think that killing myself will be my penance, I will cut my wrist right now."

"Don't you dare say that again, Shanaya!" I shouted pushing her away with my arms.

"Can you promise me one thing?" I held her hands, my eyes staring deeply into hers.

"Anything," she said with her trembling voice.

"You will never try to hurt yourself ever, promise me that. If we are meant to be together, we will get back, but just don't do anything stupid. Remember if you hurt yourself, then you are hurting me. Please don't give me more pain."

I knew that she was a very emotional person and she might do something stupid.

"I promise I will never do anything stupid. I love you," she promised with her voice loud and clear. Her face was now cheerful as if she had got some kind of hope from my promise. She cuddled me in her arms again. My hands rested at the sides. God! I wanted to hug her so much.

"Thanks. That means a lot," I whispered.

"Now, I have to go. I will drop you to a nearby auto stand," I added .

"Okay," she murmured.

ॐ

In the evening, I came back from office and ran straight to my room. For the entire day, her gloomy face repeatedly flickered in my mind. I could not focus on my work in the office, barely participating in any business discussion with my father.

Suddenly, a cloud of happy memories passed through my brain and I opened my wooden wardrobe in a quest for presents, which Shanaya had given me in these past four years.

First, I took out the chronograph watch which she had gifted on my twenty-first birthday, and then a couple of shirts which were faded due to excessive wear, a best boyfriend certificate, a colourful collage of our photographs together printed on a tile, leather belts and numerous handmade cards, which she had given to me on various occasions like our relationship anniversary, birthdays and at last the get well soon cards she made for my mother. My eyes welled up.

I picked one of the cards from the bunch; it was made with blue coloured bonded paper. On the front, a heart was marvelously made with red paper. It was an epitome of perfect craft work and creativity. In the inner page, she had written in bold letters 'Love is for life and beyond' with a colourful photograph of us, kissing each other on the lips. And then on the right bottom corner, was written in yellow glittering pen– 'Till the time sun will shine the earth, the sea is inundated with water, snow is melting away from the glaciers and cold breezes are present in the winters, I will love you with all my heart and soul'.

My lips were a hard line, I was speechless. I missed her so much. The water of the sea of my love dried up. Gazing heavenward, I folded my hands together and sent a silent prayer to god. How I wished the break-up was just a nightmare and I'd wake up again with Shanaya's morning wake up calls.

And then in the very next moment, rage took over and I wanted to burn every card she had ever made for me, but again the emotional element of my subconscious restrained me from the idea. It was unbelievable that someone who loved a person like that could be unfaithful. If I hadn't heard from her mouth that she had cheated on me, no one on this earth could have made me believe that it was true.

Desperately, I tried to escape from the tornado erupting from the gratifying reminiscences of my relationship to overwhelming, caustic reality and jumped in bed. I wanted to sleep like a baby; which was, on the contrary, not a common occurrence these days.

Never in the past six months had I woken up without having nightmares. The betrayal had taken away an essential part of me, which I was sure would be hurting for the rest of my life.

I had been trying my best to come out of the disastrous tragedy. Even though I did try to sublimate all my efforts to make my business reach heights and resumed with my German classes as well, the thoughts never stopped.

My daily calendar included waking up to the annoying sound of phone's alarm clock, which was once used to be Shanaya's sweet voice. God knew how much I missed that sweet voice! And then I would leave for work at eleven and come back at eight in the evening. Dinner was followed by long drives, mostly to and fro India Gate with Nikita. My social life, which had included only Shanaya, was packed in a suitcase and buried deep underground. Although my best friend Varun had been in touch, always persuading me to hang out and to make new friends, I never tried. Honestly, I had never shown interest.

Talking to Varun had been very comforting though, as only he and Nikita knew how much I loved Shanaya. He often came to my place just to check how I was doing.

For our time apart, not even a single day passed by without thinking about her and wondering what it would have been like if nothing had happened. But it did happen and I was still serious about not calling her. Her calls and texts were restricted, but she never gave up and continued emailing me, and asking for forgiveness.

She had figuratively broken every bit of my existence. I could not even think of getting back with her in my nightmares. And of course, I had become a misogynist. Whenever I saw a couple holding hands while strolling in the mall, it bit me in the ribs because it reminded me of her, and how perfect it had been until a few months back. I prohibited myself from going to malls, or for that matter, every place where I had been with her. Truthfully, in Delhi, there was hardly any restaurant or theater we hadn't visited together. During the weekends I made good friends in my German class. I found them very warm and friendly.

Many times in a day, I found myself sitting quietly, captivating the moments I had spent with her, the happy moments, the day I proposed to her, and the day we first made love.

I missed her smile, her dark, brown eyes in which I used to drown myself into. I missed her touch, the way she made me laugh, the way she made cards for me on my birthdays and I missed her warm hug.

♋

A few days passed. One evening I was sitting in the back seat of my car, returning from work, my eyes fixed at the ordinary shining moon, which apparently was grinning at me.

Next second, my phone buzzed. It was Varun. I smiled. I had missed him in the past few days.

"Nikhil."

"Hi, Varun. What's up?"

"Nothing much, I just came back from office. I was thinking of going out today. It's been ages since we got drunk. Let's go out," he said excitedly.

"Varun, I am not sure about that."

"Oh come on, you need to get out of your pool of sad water. You are too comfortable in it."

He had a point. For months, I had become very comfortable in cursing my life and not trying to move on.

"I will pick you in an hour or so, be ready," he ordered.

I tilted my head rolling my eyes up, contemplating whether I was ready for it or not.

"Okay, count me in," I replied indecisively.

♋

Later, in my room, I took out my favourite black t-shirt from my cupboard along with light blue denims. I was gradually getting excited as this was the first time after my break-up that I would be going out. In front of the mirror, I stood pondering over the amount of weight I had lost recently. My chest and my stomach went noticeably in. I felt confident about myself.

♋

In an hour, my phone buzzed. Varun had texted. *Come down.*

"Mom, I will be late tonight. Going out with Varun," I informed Mom who sat in front of the television watching her favourite daily soaps as I close the door behind.

"Take the spare key, Nikhil, and enjoy yourself," my mother replied smiling, sensing the excitement on my face.

Varun looked excited as this was new-fangled even for him. He wore a dark blue punk t-shirt which had 'Party Animal' printed on it which made me surreptitiously laugh at him.

"C'mon bro, let's have fun tonight!" he said as he started the engine.

We decided to go to Hauz Khas village. As per page three, it was the most happening place in town lately. The village catered to almost a hundred restaurants. It had boutiques, massage parlours, art galleries, ice cream parlours, the beautiful Hauz Khas Lake, and domed tombs of Muslim royalty. It had become one of the favourite spots for tourists.

It took us almost an hour to reach as it was Saturday and the place was crowded with party enthusiasts. Many people walked towards the restaurants and clubs, leaving their cars on the roadside to beat the heavy traffic.

♋

"Wherever we going?" I asked.

"Wherever we get entry, that's my club," he shrugged with a smirk.

"That sounds about right," I nodded, passing a smile.

"Let's start from the one on the first floor here in this building." He darted his face towards the building.

We jumped up the stairs. Our eyes widened as soon as we saw nobody at the entrance.

"Lucky day for stags, I think."

"Yeah! Let's go inside quickly before somebody stops us." He beckoned me to come up quickly. Within a split second, we scurried inside the club. I stood still squaring my shoulders.

It was darkly light up, swamped with drunk teenagers. People were dancing to Bollywood music beating loudly. It reminded me of the night out in Paris.

Varun and I looked at each other and passed a smile. We went closer to the bar.

"Two kingfishers please!" Varun requested the bartender waving his hand.

The bartender nodded, smiled and swept away behind the counter.

The moment I received the beer, I turned around and ogled at the dance floor. I drank, gasping. 'Ahh.' Too cold for my sensitive throat, I thought. It felt good and the colour returned to my face. I cleared my throat and swiped my tongue over my dry lips. Swallowing, I scanned every person in the club with an infinite slow motion. Seeing people drinking, chatting and hanging out with their friends and loved ones, fabricated an emerging ray of hope that something good would happen. After all, who knew what would happen in this long life full of twists and turns.

Contemplating on my own thoughts as I scratched my beard, I felt a piercing stare from the right. From the corner of my eye a girl, leaned back on the couch with her legs crossed near the bar, threw glances at me under her curls surreptitiously. Alone, she looked innocent in her sleeveless white top and sky blue skirt.

With a blink of an eye, I turned my neck towards the bar again as I was rather afraid of girls. In these few months, I wanted to be as far as possible from them since the one I had loved had broken my heart.

Again, I glanced towards the floor while ignoring the girl when I realized that she was looking at me again. She had exceptional forest green observant eyes and her fizzy dark brown hair hung perfectly, parted in the middle. Her nose had a couple of freckles. As my stare halted at her face, her dimples appeared from nowhere and it made her look beautiful. She was gorgeous, I must admit.

Digressing from the sight, I saw Varun talking to a girl at the other end of the bar. Damn! He has become an extrovert now, I whimpered.

From the distance, I noticed that Varun was coming towards me with that new girl.

What the hell! Why is he bringing that girl? I mumbled, taking another sip of my refreshing beer.

"Hey, Nikhil, meet Sia."

"Nikhil." I plastered a smile on my face, holding my hand out and shaking hers.

"Sia. Nice to meet you." She stroked her long hair. Five-and-a-half feet tall and counting, Sia had a very slim and lean body, and was perfectly dressed in a long red dress.

"Sia tells me that she is here with her friend and they have a table. Let's join them," Varun interrupted while clasping his drink from the bar counter.

I was in no mood to chat with strange girls, but I couldn't say no.

"Absolutely." I nodded faking a smile.

Sia directed us to her table. Lo behold! I saw that her friend was the same girl who was looking at me before. As we approached the table, Sia then introduced us to her friend.

"Hey, Ridhima, meet these guys – he is Nikhil, and this is Varun."

After the introduction, we four sat on their table on the comfortable big black leather couches.

"Hey, you guys chat, I will just get us another round of drinks with Varun," Sia said.

Ridhima and I both nodded our heads and then they both got up. I wondered whether to talk or keep my mouth shut as I had not talked to a strange girl since my break-up. She gave me a couple of stares, but I was not in a mood to initiate a chat.

"So, Nikhil, what do you do?" she queried while taking another sip of her drink, probably vodka, I guessed. Even though I was hesitant to talk, she had a positive vibe about her.

"I am looking after my family business of metals," staring down at my phone screen, I replied.

"Don't mind, but it sounds boring," she replied with a sardonic smile on her face as I raised my head up. She gripped the arms of the chair, crossing her legs.

I frowned for a moment, but then my face eased into a smile.

"Well you aren't completely wrong. But it also involves travelling to European countries twice a year to meet new people and connect with the old ones, which I found quite exciting and interesting as you meet different people and learn about their cultures and heritage," I retorted with a grin.

"I was just messing up with you. How would I know?" she smirked, playing with her hair.

"You tell me. What about you?" I asked arching my brow at her.

"Ahh, I have just completed my English honours course from Delhi University," she replied resting her chin on her hand.

"Oh. That is great, you must love literature. So, who took your heart away first?" I enquired with an inquisitive gaze.

"Excuse me? What do you mean?" she retorted, frowning at me. She blinked thrice.

"I meant your first book and the author." My hands rested on the table.

"Oh! That's a relief. I sailed towards the other side of the interpretation. It was *Hard Times* by Charles Dickens."

"Wow! That's a complete masterpiece. It's my favourite too. Even I love to read novels – romance and thrillers specifically. I used to read a lot during my early engineering days."

"An engineer, that's impressive." Her eyes narrowed as she played with her hair again with her right hand. Her soft green eyes were holding mine, kindly, but with an exciting glint.

"Is it?" I asked arching an eyebrow.

"Yes, of course, you guys are really brainy," she added.

"Thank you very much. I was thinking that you might say nerdy and boring," I said mockingly shouldering on her previous remark.

"Ha-Ha. Good one. Finally I could get a smile on your face." She laid back and briefly closed her eyes, soothingly.

"Hey guys, here are your drinks. Let's go to the dance floor," Sia interrupted.

I looked at Ridhima.

"Dance? Me? I am a terrible dancer, I can't. You guys carry on," I lied as I was in no mood to dance. I just wanted to sit and relax my brain after an exhausting day.

"Come on, Nikhil. Let's dance," Varun insisted.

"You guys go ahead and I will join you later," I said in an attempt to stop the coaxing.

"I will be waiting," he said and left with Sia.

Ridhima and I stared at both of them dancing for a considerable amount of time. They both danced quite well, especially Sia.

"I guess Varun and Sia are hitting it off."

"Yes, look at them. They are dancing like they have been dance partners for years," she replied.

"Care for another drink?" I asked hesitantly.

"Yes, please." She rubbed her hands together.

We rose and went to the bar.

"Let's take a couple of vodka shots," she requested, smoothening down her skirt.

"Geez, I am not a big aficionado of neat alcohol," I pouted.

"Oh, come on. Let's do this," she demanded.

"Okay, if you insist," I murmured.

At the bar, we knocked out two vodka shots each in ten seconds while sucking lemon desperately to nullify vodka's strong aftertaste and burning as it goes down the food pipe. Her body shook as alcohol went down her throat.

"Yuck! Are you happy now?" I asked with a grin.

"Very much."

"What?" I asked.

"I am slammed now; finally, the party has begun."

"Another round?" she asked inching closer, almost shouting in my ear as the music was loud.

"No, please. Maybe after some time."

"So, Ridhima, tell me more about yourself," I asked.

"Umm, I am the only child."

"Oh! A single child, pampered for sure."

She briefly touched her nose. "You have no idea Nikhil," she took a deep breath and looked down at her hands as she let out a sigh.

"That's great."

Shaking her head, she said, "I was being sarcastic, Nikhil. My parents are workaholics as they are both top-notch lawyers."

"Hmm. I am sorry, Ridhima," I nodded empathetically.

"You don't have to be." She bit her lip in thought.

"Anyway, I have applied for Master's in English Literature to Oxford."

Suddenly, her voice was full of enthusiasm and a smile appeared on her face.

"Brilliant, man! That's awesome, all the best," I exclaimed impatiently. "I wish I could study in Europe."

"You want to pursue that course?" she eyed me speculatively.

"No, but I wanted to go to Germany for Master's in Automobile Engineering."

"Then why did you drop out?" Her eyes flamed, filled with curiosity.

"My family was not convinced," I replied gazing towards the floor.

"So you gave up on that opportunity?" she said with wide eyes keeping her hand on the side of her forehead.

"Yes," I gasped as I didn't want to tell her the actual reason.

We conversed for another half an hour. There was something about her that made me feel comfortable talking to her.

"I should be going now, it's almost one," she squinted at her wrist watch.

"Okay, I waved to Varun on the dance floor, insinuating him to come back. "What happened Nikhil?"

"Ridhima is saying that they have to go. I think we should also be going."

"I guess you are right," he retorted.

We walked out of the club and stepped downstairs.

"Ridhima, you can note down my phone number and message me when you reach home safely."

"I am going with my driver, Nikhil. Don't worry. But I must say that's a nice way to ask a girl's phone number," she said giving me a playful smile.

I giggled and typed my number on her phone. She instantly gave me a missed call.

"It was nice meeting you, Nikhil. Bye," she said smiling.

"Same here. Bye, Ridhima."

"Blue eyes, nice meeting you," I wished Sia as we shook hands.

Ridhima threw a bizarre glance at me. And they walked towards the car.

They both sat in Ridhima's car together – a car with a red VIP light on top.

"I hope I am not getting myself into trouble," I mumbled jokingly.

And then we headed towards my car.

"I think you had a pretty nice time," I said taking another step.

"I am glad that I came today. I really like Sia. What about you?"He turned his face towards me.

"It was okay. Finally, I was out for a change."

"We should do it more often. Did you ask her for her number?" Varun enquired.

"I did."

"Ayee! Somebody got lucky tonight."

"It's not like that, just that there is no harm making some new friends."

"And what about you?"

"I am taking her out next Saturday," he said raising his hand high for a high-five.

"Nice," I replied as I went for a high-five up in the air.

♋

It was 2 a.m. and I hit the sack as soon as I reached. I was trying to sleep when my phone beeped. I grabbed the phone kept on the side table of my bed and found an email from Shanaya. Indecisively, I patted my fingers on my phone screen, but finally, I opened the email, as I was missing her. I wondered why she was awake this late. I found a long poem, which I tried to read opening my bleary eyes.

I gave you the pain no one can possibly give
But believe me, that was just not me
If life bestows me another chance,
To feel, to give back what you have always given me
I just want to drown in the sea of your love
Because without you, its water is getting all red
Baby, I wish you will forgive me and take me in your arms
Because I want to feel… Feel your love again

With the rise of sun to the fall,
What you have always given me is your unconditional love,
The way your words quiver my inner soul,
The shiver that I feel running down my spine with your touch,
Your voice has always been music to my ears,
Your eyes manifested how much you loved me
I miss that smile on my face whenever I was with you
Baby, I wish you will forgive me because I want to smile like that again
I want to feel… Feel your love again

When I first met you, my heart sank in your ocean of eternal, profound and endless love

My heart pounded outside my chest
My impenetrable heart was not mine anymore
Because it felt your love before I did
As you filled my heart with the joys of the spring, I was walking on air
Baby, I wish you will forgive me and take me through those waters
Because I want to feel... Feel your love again

Remember the way you took care of me
When I was under the weather
The way your body responded to my every heartbeat,
I was not an angel but you made feel like one,
And I blew it by mistake,
Please, baby, give me another chance and give me another tour of your love
Because I want to feel... Feel your love again

And now since you are not here, with every breath I take, my heart squeezes in pain,
And it's not going to happen for long, as I can see myself fading away
Forgive me one last time please and take me along on this journey of life
I beg you; forgive me one last time,
Because, Baby, I want to live your love again... all over again.

Your love,
Shanaya

With every word I read, tears fell like water from a tap. I could imagine the pain she was going through from every single word she wrote, but a slight thought of getting back with her sent tremors down my body as I couldn't trust her anymore.

Even though I was still mad at her, my soul wanted to be loved again. After all, I couldn't forget her for the rest of my life.

My soul was desperate to know how she was doing. Was she fine? Was she eating well or whether her blood pressure was normal as it always stayed on the lower side. I wanted to see how she looked now. I wanted to meet her and hug her so that I could survive for at least the next few months. I was wandering in the stream of my thoughts while my phone beeped again. It was a text from Ridhima informing me that she had reached home. I immediately replied to her.

I really had fun today. Good night.

I covered my face with the white soft blanket and closed my eyes. I was able to think about the night out. The memories calmed my nerves and I could feel my eyelids gradually closing.

Next afternoon, I was watching a movie with my sister at the nearby theatre. It was a love story between two cancer patients who fall in love during chemotherapy. As the movie progressed, my emotions towards it had escalated from boredom to a point of depression.

"Ahhh!" I let out a frustrated sigh.

Firstly, all the scenes involved medical equipment, doctors, chemotherapy sessions and so on, and reminded me of the painful period when my mother was ill. Secondly, their true love stroked a chord of what I still felt for Shanaya.

Bored stiff, I took my phone out of my pocket. After tapping a few buttons, I read Ridhima's name on the lock screen. Impatiently, I opened her message.

What's up? Can we meet in the evening?

"Really?" I mumbled to myself. My eyes widened. We had just met and she wanted to meet again. Though sceptical, I asked myself, why not? I am not doing anything after the movie anyway.

I typed quickly. *I am watching a movie with my sister. Yes, we can meet.*

As I pressed the sent button, I gazed at the movie screen again and felt an overwhelming emotion penetrating my brain. To distract my mind, I checked my phone again. Ridhima was quick.

She had replied. *Starbucks, Greater Kailash at six, ok?*

With a half-smile on my face, I typed. *Sounds good.*

♋

An hour later, the movie had ended. Thank God! I mumbled.

"You didn't like it?" Nikita asked, turning her face towards me, her expressions tight.

"No love stories in hospitals for me, please." I showed a dismissive finger.

"Yes, it was a bit depressing." She tilted her head and continued. "By the way, where were you last night?" she asked pointedly.

"I just went out for a couple of drinks with Varun," I responded getting up from the seat.

"Ok. I hope you had fun. It's good to see you going out for a change," she said and smiled.

♋

At Starbucks, I sat comfortably in my chair beside the freshly polished table carrying the annoying heady scent of spirits. My head leaned on the back and arms rested on the sides. I glanced at the wrist watch, it said fifteen past six. I looked around me. For the first time in almost six months, I was comfortable being around people. Most importantly, I could bear couples around me now.

After a brief second, from the distance, I saw Ridhima coming towards me. She threw an apologetic smile.

"Sorry to keep you waiting," she apologized.

"It's okay." I smiled and pulled out a chair for her.

"I am glad you came, I was bored alone at home," she said as she parked herself.

"I was bored too." I restricted myself from telling her about the movie. "What about your parents? It's Sunday, they must be home?" I asked.

"No, they are out somewhere, probably in a meeting with a client." She rolled her eyes.

"Okay. What about Sia? Did she stay at your place?"

"Are you trying to say that I made a mistake asking you to meet me?" she said acidly, scowling back at me. "Why such a series of questions?" She was exasperated now.

"I am sorry. I was just curious," I smirked, staring into her eyes.

"You don't know me well enough to torture me like that, mister," she said with a lopsided grin on her face.

"Relax, please. I have a tendency to jest with people feel comfortable with," I said while making the peace sign with my hands.

"Ha-Ha. You know what, I am really short tempered," she giggled.

"I can see that," I responded rolling my eyes away from her face, hoping that she would not vent her anger on me. I was enjoying messing with her. Her fun-loving nature made me want to talk to her more.

"You are doing that again," she frowned and a corner of her mouth lifted.

"I am sorry, but I find it amusing to pull your leg like that."

"Stop it, Nikhil. Come on!"

I waved to the waiter to take the order in a much-needed attempt to digress and cool her off.

"What will you have? I asked her softly.

"I will have cold coffee with two spoons of sugar," she ordered.

"What about you, sir?" The waiter turned towards me.

"Same please."

"So tell me more about yourself, Nikhil," she asked running her hand through her hair as a smile swept her face.

Not being sure on what to say, I started by being humorous.

"Well, I am quite an introvert and do not have a tendency to make many friends." I smirked.

"Ya right, don't mock me; you are not an introvert, for god's sake," she grinned wickedly.

"Hey, how could you figure that out?" I put my hands on the table.

"An introvert does not interact with strange girls and goes out for a coffee the very next day."

"Ahah. That's a considerable point, but Varun initiated it yesterday."

"Whatever," she held her palm out to me.

"Do you have a girlfriend?" she asked intriguingly.

I was not sure whether to answer her question honestly.

"What do you think?" I asked dramatically, trying to be serious.

"I can't say." She looked away embarrassed.

The waiter came and put down our coffees on the table.

"No, I don't have any girlfriend now." I revealed. "And you?"

She pressed her lips together. Suddenly her face saddened.

"I never liked anyone in that way."

It was quite difficult to believe. There must be something behind her lonely past, I thought, as pretty girls are always approached by boys.

"And what do you mean by you don't have a girlfriend *now?*" she asked as she took a sip of her coffee.

"Well, I am not yet over my ex," I replied folding my hands on my chest.

"Hmm. So we have something important to discuss." Her smile was back again.

"No, I don't want to talk about it," I replied.

"Oh come on, at least tell me what happened, and why did you guys break up?" She sat upright and put her hands on her waist.

After a long time, I was having fun while talking to someone and I did not want to ruin it.

"Let's not. I don't want to pour my heart out today."

"I am sure you will be back with her again since you still miss her so much," she claimed.

"Enough of me, why haven't you been in a serious one?" I asked her.

She propped her chin on her palm. She looked confused and short of words.

"Honestly, I never found someone worthy of risking my heart over."

She leaned back in her chair and looked away.

"That's interesting," I replied cocking my head towards the right.

"It is rather sad." She rolled her eyes at me and stared at her coffee.

"Don't say that. Okay tell me, who would be your kind of guy?" I asked.

"Nothing specific, I should get the feeling from the gut," she answered.

"I like how you think. There will always be a lot of pressure to your gut then." I laughed holding my stomach.

"Stop it, you moron. Ha-Ha." Her dimples were back and I smiled.

After an hour, we finally decided to leave. She was a good listener, but she was garrulous as well, which is just opposite of what I am.

I extended my hand for a handshake, but she misread, swept closer and gave me a side hug.

"Goodbye, Nikhil. Let's meet on Saturday if you are free," she whispered.

"I will let you know. Bye," I mumbled hugging her back.

♋

"Nikhil, what are you doing, son?" My father asked while I was checking my accounts at the month end, sitting in my office chair scratching my head.

"Dad, I was just calculating the outcome of this month and I found out that we made no profit this month. In fact, we incurred a loss," I replied.

"I know, Nikhil. With this global plummeting of metal prices, our sales are down and the prices are constantly decrementing," he said empathetically pulling a chair.

"I think we should stop buying new material for the time being and let the market stabilize."

"It's a very good idea, Nikhil, and I must tell you with this market volatility, I don't see it stabilizing in the near future," he said rubbing his upper lip.

"Let's slow down business for a couple of months then," I concluded.

He nodded agreeing, stood up and walked out of the office.

It had been a very stressful month as I tried to negotiate with my clients for a good selling price; nonetheless, as the market was not favourable, my hard work didn't pay off. I was constantly under trauma, thinking about the loss and how I could turn things around.

I was lying on my bed after dinner with my arms behind my neck as my mind travelled from one thought to the other. And every thought ended up with a picture of me holding hands with Shanaya. It was her positivity towards life that always used to lift me up whenever I felt low.

"Every time I feel low, I think about you and my life is awesome again," I recalled what I used to say to her back in the day. Darn, I missed her so much! She was the best thing that had happened to me and then life took her away. I was sure that if I had her in this gloomy phase of my life, it would have made a huge difference because when I would talk, I forgot all my worrries. A thought entered my mind and I quickly opened my mailbox on my phone.

I scrolled down and then finally in my spam folder, I found a few emails sent by her the previous day. I clicked on the most recent email. She had typed everything which she had done the day before: when she woke up, what she did the whole day, and how she misses me. She ended her email apologizing.

Her emails staggered my nerves. Was she still hoping that sooner or later we would get back together? God! I envied her optimism. "She just never gives up," I mumbled looking upwards towards the ceiling. I nodded off to sleep with my phone in my hand.

The next day, in the afternoon, I was working in my office with a pen gliding on my lips, when my phone beeped.

It was a text message from Ridhima.

Strangers Club at 9. Sia and Varun are also coming.

I shook my head saying a silent no.

Not today. I am not in a mood to go out.

After sending the message, I kept my phone on the table and continued reading the contracts that had recently matured.

My phone vibrated on the table again. It was her.

I am not asking you. I am ordering you ;)

A smile lit up my face. Had our friendship really walked so far? It had been a month now since we first met each other.

As we met every weekend for dinner or for clubbing, we did get closer. Although Sia and Varun had always been there, we always ended up talking to each other and sharing many things about our past and college days. Many times, in the day, I found myself texting her out of no reason, sometimes just sending a tongue teaser smiley on WhatsApp and we ended up chatting for hours. Also, there were days when we talked exchanging just the emoticons. She had a tendency to lift up my mood whenever I was sad, the same way Shanaya had always done. Along with some happy memories of my past relationship with Shanaya, I even told her the true reason why I didn't go to Germany. One thing I never shared with her was why Shanaya and I had broken up.

♋

"Hey look, there! Let's park the car here," I suggested, pointing my finger towards a vacant space just outside a restaurant, my head darting out of the window.

"I am not sure whether they will let us park here since we are not going to this restaurant."

Varun was right. It was never easy to find car parking on Saturday nights in Connaught Place.

"Dude, it's thirty minutes past nine and Ridhima has called thrice. I have just texted her that we are coming in a minute."

"Ok, let's park here quickly then."

Varun parked the car and hastily we walked towards the club.

As we stepped closer to the club, I saw Ridhima standing at the entrance with her hands fixed on her waist. She looked furious, her face flushed.

I ran my eyes over her as I stepped closer. She was looking beautiful in a short, thigh length red dress which highlighted her fair and glossy legs.

"I've been standing here for the last thirty minutes," she said angrily.

"Hey, Ridhima, are you planning to burn this place or what? You look so hot!"

I deliberately complimented her to cool her off.

"Shut up!"

"I am sorry and don't you dare talk to me like that when you look so beautiful, it's unbecoming."

Her expression loosened up and her lips widened. She was charmed by the compliment, I could tell.

"I am sorry too, Ridhima," Varun interrupted.

"I am sorry," I said again.

"It's okay. Let's go, Sia is inside."

There was a magnificent square shaped bar counter at the heart, with three sides sitting area with huge dusky leather couches and dance floor on one side. Luckily the music was not that loud since we had come in early, but a few couples and a group had already started dancing.

As we came in, I saw Sia coming towards us with a gentle smile on her face. She hugged Varun and he pecked a kiss on her lips.

Wow! That's the first time I had seen him kissing a girl. Ridhima and I exchanged looks with a frown.

"Hi Sia, how are you?" I asked as they drew apart.

"I am good, Nikhil. How are you?"

"Great." I nodded smiling.

Later we walked towards the bar and ordered a few drinks. The club gradually got deluged with people mostly of our age, but there were a few elder couples who were just sitting quietly at their table drinking unobtrusively and appreciating the music. I was gulping another sip of Jack Daniels – my favourite whiskey – when abruptly Shanaya's face flickered in front of my eyes. Damn! Her gorgeous body in my arms swaying with mine would have been a moment in paradise. Like a ghost, I went to my table staggering away from the crowd and kept my drink on the table.

I was sitting alone with a hand on my cheek, head tilted, contemplating on how life had changed with time. After a couple of minutes, Ridhima walked towards me and sat next to me. Due to the deafening music now, her voice was not perceptible so she nudged me as she spoke.

"What happened? Why did you come here?" she asked.

"Nothing."

"Anything bothering you, Nikhil?"

From where should I start? I thought.

"I had a hectic day."

"Anything you want to share?" she asked while gently putting one hand on my shoulder

"Umm..."

"That's the problem with you, Nikhil. You don't open up easily. Every time, I have to force you," she whined. She leaned back, her hands crossed over her chest.

"I don't know what exactly, but I feel life has been really hard on me. Two years ago, I was living life king size, happy and satisfied in whatever god has given me. Suddenly one day everything changed. It seems like god is taking everything away from me. In addition, Shanaya is all over my mind since the past few days." I closed my eyes, tilting my head back.

"Ohh. If you both still love each other, then why don't you guys get back together?"

Like that would have been an option. She is so naive, I pondered.

"It's easier said than done. Things are way more complicated now," I responded.

"We were just right together – companionable, understanding each other completely and all, but she screwed everything. Anyway, I don't want to bore you, so let's not talk about it."

"No, I want to hear everything. Tell me what you are thinking right now."

With the chambers of my heart wide open, I said, "Right now, I am missing her smile. Last year, it was the second day of her period and she was not feeling well at night. To make her feel good, I went to meet her the very next morning, skipping college, with her favourite ice cream and chocolates.

"I can't tell you, but she had the most beautiful smile on her face when she saw me and it was priceless. I am missing that beautiful smile that had kept me going and helped me face any problem in life."

I inched forward and grabbed my drink. I was parched. I took one large sip and then leaned back and continued, "Another time, it was her birthday and I planned a surprise birthday party for her. I coordinated with all her friends for a week and persuaded her friends to come to the party. I had decorated the entire restaurant with balloons and party ribbons with small cards pasted on the walls that I had made for her. She was so happy that day. I want to see her smiling again. I want her."

Ridhima seemed dumbfounded.

"You know Ridhima, if it's for her, I can do anything in life." I put my hands on my head. Damn! I missed her.

"She is really a lucky girl." Awe transformed her face.

"Nikhil, I must tell you that you are an ideal boyfriend and definitely will be a perfect husband."

"I am not so sure about that," I responded shaking my head.

"One thing I often wonder about is why would she let go of a guy like you, because honestly, I wish I could find someone like you. Who can cheer me up when I feel low, who can go distances just for my smile, the one who takes care of me when I am sick. That would have been like a dream come true." She laughed.

"You are just being polite. She also loved me with all her heart. She always used to wake me up in the morning whenever I had to go somewhere. You can now comprehend why I am always late," I chuckled.

She laughed.

"Whenever I got late at night, she waited for me so that we could talk, even if she was sleepy. She always held me up when I felt low. I miss being with her, being loved again," I added.

"She was always so caring. Whenever I had a headache, she gave me head massages, and you know what, her magical fingers always soothed my pain."

"Magical fingers, really?" She laughed extending her fingers apart looking at them.

"It was magical because it was hers. My body responds to her differently."

"Whatever she used to do, it was wonderful because she did it..." I added.

"But one thing that still bothers me is why you guys broke up," she interrupted me.

I held my head in my hands again. I bit my lip, trying to hold the wet pain that threatened my eyes. I couldn't hold them back.

"Ridhima, she lik... liked somebody else," I stammered while sobbing.

"What? Damn! That's not right, how could she?" she frowned, and her mouth fell open. She started biting her fingertips.

"I don't know. The day I got to know about it, I didn't look back. But now she is after me to forgive her as she realizes her mistake," I said.

"Nikhil, look at me!" she hollered as she held my hands to console me.

I raised my head and glanced towards her.

"She does not deserve your love, and you have to forgive her and move on, for your peace. You will feel better, trust me."

"How could she?" I whined with my tears dropping. "Life has been so hard these two years."

"Nikhil, it will get better soon."

"How would you know? Rich parents, an only child. Step into my shoes once. You will feel the pain."

"You think I have an easy and perfect life?" she shouted slamming her hands on her thighs.

"You tell me if I am wrong."

"Come, I will show you how life has been easy on me. And wipe your tears," She said bitterly as she held my hand tightly.

I panicked looking into her eyes. I wiped my tears.

We rose up from the seat and she pulled me behind her.

"Wait a minute, I am coming back."

She went in. There I was, standing on my feet outside the ladies washroom, completely baffled about why she had dragged me there.

After a couple of seconds, she opened the door and pulled me inside. 'Come quickly.'

She took me to one closed partition and slammed the door.

"What the hell are you up to Ridhima?"

"Whatever I am telling you today should never come out of your heart."

"Okay," I nodded.

She closed her eyes and took a deep breath.

She gently took off one shoulder of her dress looking away from me, followed by the other one.

"What are you doing, why are you removing your clothes?"

She pulled her dress down to her breast.

"Let me tell you what I've been going through since the last ten years."

"Do you see this?" she pointed towards her breast.

I lowered my head and saw her red brazier. I was in a state of shock when I saw an ugly scar just over her breast.

"What is this?"

"This is the truth of my life that I had been hiding from you and from everybody I have ever known."

"I don't understand."

"Ten years ago, my parents got separated. They both being lawyers had a very strong opinion on every aspect of life. Down the line, they realized that they couldn't live together anymore."

I took a deep breath.

"My mother moved in with her ex-boyfriend from college along with me. To say the least, he was not a decent man. He used to drink the entire day and had no shame or any sort of respect for women. One day I was sleeping in my mother's room when he came and threw away my bed sheet and sat over me. I cried, yelled for help but he tried to rip off my clothes. He stared at me with eyes full of lust and tried to rape me," she continued.

My heart was no longer beating at a human pace.

"By luck, I got hold of a night lamp from the side table and smashed it on his head when he was about to enter me." She pressed her eyes closed and trembled.

"He bled and got furious. Suddenly he pulled out a knife from his pocket and pierced my breast saying that this mark would never let me live a happy life and I'd remember him whenever I'd see this."

My mouth gaped. All I could do was stare at that ugly zig-zag scar.

"And he was right, I do remember him every day I bathe."

"Stop it!" I shouted keeping my hands on her shoulders. The pain I felt in my head was unbearable. Her face had dried up.

"Every day I wake up with this horror, now tell me, whose life is harder?" she asked with her eyebrows raised.

"I am sorry, I didn't know," my voice grew louder.

"We moved back to my dad's house the very next day."

I closed the lid of the toilet and sat down with my shoulders sagging. My mind was blocked. My body trembled.

I couldn't believe that even after she had gone through so much of torture, and that too in her early teens, she still put up such a happy face. I raised my head and looked into her eyes. They were moist.

Once again, I lowered my head. Her eyes were inundated with so much pain that I couldn't take it anymore.

Suddenly, I felt Ridhima's hand on my shoulder, I looked up and found her leaning towards me. She sat on my lap.

"What are you doing Ridhima?"

"Don't say anything, let me hug you please," she requested and her arms were around my back.

Although, it felt weird since she hugged me for the very first time, but she was my good friend now and I wanted to make her feel better. My hands went around her back sympathetically.

As much as she tried to hold it in, the pain came out thrashing the rusty doors of her past in the form of a scream. Her tears burst like water from a dam. Her grip tightened against my back. I blinked my lashes which were now heavy with tears.

"I am sorry Ridhima. I wish I could take your pain away."

She pulled herself back a little and stared deep into my eyes. Her eyes were sad and I couldn't bear the sadness spread on her face. Immediately, I glanced away. She suddenly held my head from behind and pressed her lips on mine. My eyes widened and drowned to nothingness.

Her insistent mouth parted my trembling lips. Her lips tasted like vanilla which evolved wild tremors along my nerves.

My mind betrayed me and I found myself kissing her back. Maybe to take her pain away. Every moment, there was something from the back of my mind that told me that I was crossing the limits.

"You have me, Ridhima. I will be your friend till the end of time. Stop crying, please."

The moment I heard the word 'friend', I felt a hammer being hit hard on my head.

What the hell am I doing? I questioned myself. I still love Shanaya. This is not friendship, I mumbled. In a wink, I pushed Ridhima away.

"I am sorry, I have to go. This is so wrong."

Ridhima stood up. She was embarrassed.

"I am sorry Nikhil," she apologized wiping her tears.

"It's okay, but I have to go," I said shaking my head. I never knew I could degrade myself to such a level. I felt like I had cheated on Shanaya. Or rather I had cheated on my love. I was unfaithful to it. How could I kiss another girl when the queen of my heart still lived in it?

I rose up as quickly as possible, unbolted the door and left the washroom.

My jaw twitched when a low crackle of thunder made its way into my room through the open window, breaking the silence. I jumped out of my study chair, elated, and stepped closer towards the window. As I looked outside, it occurred to me that something was amiss. Above in the sky, black clouds loomed threateningly. The cold wind brushed against me even as another crackle of thunder rent the air. As I gazed at the street leaning against the window with a hand on my neck, I saw people running around, opening their umbrellas. I took a deep breath. It was evident that the rains would be bountiful. It wasn't for long when I saw lightning zap through the sky. The downpour started. I heard the rain drops drumming against the canopy. Pleased, I extended my hand out of the window and felt the cold water on my hands. They refreshed my thoughts, bringing an unexpected smile on my face.

"Damn! I want to go out and get drenched in the rain," I wished.

For the last one hour, I had been staring at my wall clock repeatedly as I could not concentrate. I was trying to study for my German language exam due next Sunday. To say the least, the gorgeous weather outside did no justice to my distressing meditative thoughts. The rain signified an imminent change.

My mind raced back and forth from German vocabulary to my last meeting with Ridhima.

She had become a very good friend now and something this unfortunate had happened to her was tough to digest. For the first time in my life, I felt that growing up is a curse. Everyone portrayed the best things about life to you in early days, but when you grew up slowly, you acquainted yourself with the cruel and hideous realities of this world. My problems appeared like a small stone in front of a gigantic mountain. Last night when she hugged me, I wanted to comfort her and make her feel that I would be there for her forever. Her scar never left my mind for a second. In addition, I was feeling guilty for kissing her back. It was not the right thing to do, and I knew it.

She had stolen away a magnificent space in my heart. Apparently, she was the strongest woman I had ever met. Being tortured every second by her dark unfaithful past, she stood as strong as a pillar. It was evident that I would be learning many things from her through my travels through this crazy, little thing called life.

Finally, I decided to not think about her and returned to my study table.

I was determined to score well this time. It had been my tendency to procrastinate when it came to studies, and in the last two months, I had not even opened the book once and had hardly attended any classes.

Seconds later, my phone beeped. I threw an interested eye towards the screen and saw Ridhima's name blinking on it.

Damn! What would I say if she asks me why I ran like that? I muffled, terrified.

Swallowing, I grabbed my phone and tapped on the green button as I stood up.

"Hi." Her voice was fresh.

"*Hallo! Guten Morgen Herren*," I deliberately replied to her in German. Not being sure why I did it, but I just didn't want her to start a serious conversation.

"What language is this? And what does it mean?" she asked clearly surprised.

"It's German and it means 'good morning ma'am," I responded quickly.

"Ha-Ha. Don't flaunt your German," she replied laughing.

I sighed as she sounded fine.

"I am just practicing as I have my German exam next week."

"Okay. I am sorry for yesterday, Nikhil. I may have crossed a line."

"I am sorry too, Ridhima. Also, I should not have left the club like that."

"It's okay. Can we meet tonight?"

Her words felt sharp like an arrow to my forehead. Oh god! I was not ready to talk to her about yesterday as I was full of guilt because I had no possible explanation about why I kissed her back and what if she misunderstood my feelings. I was scared about what this might lead to.

"I can't. I have my German exam next Sunday."

"Are you sure that's the only reason?" she asked, coming straight to the point.

"Yes. I haven't studied from months and I can study only on weekends as I have office the rest of the week."

"Nikhil, I am sure you are not avoiding me because of what happened yesterday or because of my past. I hope it will not affect our friendship."

My mouth gaped when her words entered my earholes. I couldn't believe that she looked so down on me. Some drunk guy had forced himself on her, so what? It was not her fault. On the contrary, for me, she was a superstar now.

"No, Ridhima, why would you say something like that? I am sorry if you felt so from my behaviour. Secondly, we are friends, we had a moment and we kissed. That was all." Disappointed, I sat down on my chair again.

"Don't be sorry. Okay, we will meet next Sunday then."

"Sure, bye."

"Okay, all the very best," she said and soon disconnected.

Phew! I sighed. That could have been worse.

♋

"Yay! No more exams!" I exclaimed taking an over excited breath, wiping the drop of sweat from my forehead, while walking out of the examination room. It was Sunday afternoon and my exam had gone unexpectedly well. For the first time, I was less nervous and not at all short of breath in front of the examiner. As I walked towards my car, I remembered that I had promised Ridhima that I'd meet her. Throughout the week, she did not even text me once, neither did I. I pulled my car door, sat down, and rang her.

"Hey, how you doing?" I asked putting my phone on the loudspeaker and started the engine.

"Hi, I am good. How was your exam?"

"It was unexpectedly great," I replied.

"Bravo! Anyway, Nikhil, I have to tell you something. Can you meet me tonight?"

"Tonight, umm…"

"It's important, Nikhil."

"So, what is it you wanna tell me?" I asked completely amazed.

"I will tell you over dinner," she replied.

"Come on, at least give a clue," I insisted.

"Later, bye," she replied and disconnected the phone.

As I hung up the phone, my mind was constantly deliberating about what she had to tell me. My mind could find out only two possibilities. Either she had heard some good news from Oxford University, where she had applied for Master's, or she wanted to talk about what happened the other day. I would have to wait and see.

♋

I panted outside the restaurant trying to catch my breath, keeping my hands on my knees. Damn! How do I get late every time? I grumbled. I squinted towards my wrist watch. I was thirty minutes late.

I stood straight and walked in. The restaurant was already packed and I looked around everywhere, but couldn't find her. I hoped that she hadn't left. Then, I turned my gaze to the extreme left corner and saw her sitting far away from the crowd. She looked up, her eyes caught mine and they were sad. Sad beyond words. Running my eyes over her blue full sleeved top and black skirt as I made my way towards the table, my mind pondered whether she looked extremely beautiful today or all this while but I hadn't noticed it.

"Sorry for being late," I said, pulling a chair.

"Don't be. I know you can never be on time," she muttered.

I could see something really swirling in her head. She looked miserable. With her arms resting on her lap, shoulders sagging and face pale, her body language spoke volumes.

"I want to tell you something, Nikhil," she said picking up a glass of water from the table taking a large sip.

"Yeah, I know. But first, you have to tell me a secret."

There was a feeling in my gut that said that she didn't get admission. I wanted to cheer her up before she told me the bad news. So, I tried something that had worked for me throughout my life.

"What now?" She raised an eyebrow as she kept her hands together on the table.

"How do you manage to look so pretty every time?" I leaned back in my chair, smiling.

As expected, her face broke into a wide smile. Wow, she really had a beautiful smile.

"Stop it already. I am not looking that good. But I must say your compliments always manage to bring a smile on my face," she commented. There! At least for a moment, her smile was back! My subconscious figuratively gave me a round of applause.

"I am hungry. What will you prefer: Chinese or North Indian?" I requested.

"Nikhil, wait, I have to tell you something first." Her lips were a hard line now.

"Yes, please tell me."

She inched closer, crossing her legs. Her eyes blocked my sight. I stared down at her knuckles. Words failed her repeatedly, I could tell.

"Do you remember about Oxford?"

Holy shit! I had guessed correctly.

"Yes, did you get any response from them?" I asked acting normal, as by her face I could tell that she hadn't got admission.

"They replied."

"And?" My teeth almost bit my tongue. My heart abruptly thumped faster with my eyes brimming with concern.

"I got selected," she revealed as she looked down again, staring at her fingers now.

"What? Shit, that's such great news; I am so happy for you. You scared me today, Ridhima."

Wow! She did get admission. Why the hell was she sad then?

I jumped from my seat and put my arms around her to congratulate her, but she didn't move a hair.

"Please, wait. I have to tell you something more, sit down," she requested.

"Oh, what else?" I sat down with my elbows on the table.

"I don't want to go now," she murmured.

'What was she up to?' I was confused.

"Why not? It was your dream, remember? Don't be stupid." With a frown, my reply was instant.

She raised her head, her gaze discomforting, eyeballs fixed as if she was casting a spell on me.

"This is harder than I thought." She bit her lower lip.

"What now, Ridhima? We are friends, you can tell me anything." I gently squeezed her hand over the table. She raised her head up.

"Nik... Nikhil... I..." She stammered taking a harsh breath, tears sparkled in her eyes. She drew her lower lip between her teeth.

"Nikhil, I love you. I want to spend the rest of my life with you."

I blinked owlishly. My mouth widened and I stared at her motionless. The colour drained out from my face. Certainly, I was not expecting her to say what she just did. I couldn't move; a vein popped out of my neck. Gosh! My lips had gone rigid and a thunderstorm of emotions swept my mind away.

"Ridhima, you don't love me; you just met me a couple of months ago," I huffed.

"Don't tell me what I feel." She scowled at me plunging her hands on the table and continued. "When I am with you, my heart smiles; every time I see you, I feel like hugging you. That day when you held me in your arms, my life changed. It felt like home Nikhil; the home I never had, full of love and life. And when I kissed you, I felt like I was walking in heaven. I never felt something like that with anyone ever. After ten years, I am finally so happy and I thank god that I have met you. In these last two months, I have fallen for you Nikhil. And then there's a feeling in my gut that if I don't tell you now, then we will be lost in this big bad world. With you, I feel safe and I feel happy."

I blinked twice and said nothing. I tried again and queried, "What about your dream?"

"Nikhil, we cannot have everything in life. My dream stands nowhere if I have a choice to be with you. Because of my unfaithful past, I have never trusted any guy in my life. But when it comes to you, it's all different," she confessed taking a tentative sip of water.

My mouth had dried up. I extended my hand forward and clasped my fingers around her glass and gulped the water till it was finished. Nervously, I began tapping my fingers on the table.

"I can't let you go, Nikhil. I can leave everything for you. Please understand," Ridhima squeezed my hand as a tear dropped out from her eye.

Still stunned by her words, I took the liberty of being patient.

"Are you going to leave me hanging or what? Please say something," she requested, pressing my hand harder.

She had become my good friend and I couldn't hurt her or promise anything which I could never fulfill. For me, Shanaya was everything. She was all over me still, in every part of my existence. How could I forget her and move on? What if I could never forget her? What if I died being single? Overcome with random thoughts, my mind was a chaos now.

"Ridhima, you are a very nice girl, very beautiful and you have a very pretty heart, but you know I love Shanaya. I always have and I always will," I said trying very hard not to hurt her.

"Nikhil, but you guys have been apart for so long. We can try to work things out. I am sure gradually you will love me back as we are so good together. You can take as much time as you want. There is no rush." She swallowed hard to prevent herself from crying. I watched the pain flashing in her eyes. It was unbearable.

"Ridhima, I am sure that this is just infatuation."

"Nikhil," she tasted my name on her tongue and tears blurted through her eyes. God! She was hurt by my words now.

"I just want you to be with me for the rest of my life. You can name it anything you want. You can call it attraction, crush, infatuation or whatever. But only I know what I feel for you. You know, since the day I have met you, whenever my phone rings, every single time, I hope it is your name that appears on the screen. I just love the way you look at me with respect. The most important thing for me is that I trust you with my life and my heart. I know I am safe in your arms and you will protect me. And when you touch me, I forget that the rest of the world even exists. If you need to hear why I love you, I can go on all night."

I was completely overwhelmed by whatever she said. She had convinced me with her words that she actually loved me. I knew I liked her too. After all, she was a gem of a person – audacious, beautiful, intelligent, caring and had a most beautiful heart. But sometimes it's just hard to love somebody. In life, it's amazing how someone just so perfect comes your way and is willing to love you just the way you are.

If I hadn't loved Shanaya, I was sure I would have fallen for her.

I shook my head rolling my eyes from her to the people sitting on the adjacent table. How should I make her understand that I could not love anyone other than Shanaya?

"Anybody will fall in love with you, Ridhima, but you know my case. I just can't give it to you. I am damaged," I said as I rubbed my hand on her cheek. She nodded slowly as if she wanted to understand my point of view.

"Nikhil, please give it a try." Ridhima stopped my hand on her cheek.

"It's not you. I am the problematic one here; please understand and you are my very good friend. I don't want to betray or lie to you. And I am really sorry if I have misled you."

She removed her hand from mine agitatedly and appeared very hurt.

I was feeling bad for her. My heart had a place only for one girl in my life. Whether she was with me or not, my heart would only beat for her.

"I don't understand," she snorted, "you don't even want to get back with her, but still you don't want to give us a chance? It's my fault, for a change I thought my life will be beautiful because you were in it. I think I just can't dream anymore because it won't come true."

"Ridhima, we are friends and always will be," I said.

"I can't be just friends with you now. I want more. I want all of you. I want your arms wrapped around me for the rest of my life." Her voice had confidence and it was clear that she wanted more. I walked down the memory lane when I had said the same words to Shanaya. It made me recall how I had felt before: pathetic and awful. Avoiding eye contact with her, I looked down and remained quiet.

"Uff! your silence is killing me Nikhil, just tell me honestly if you didn't feel anything for me just for a second, then why the hell did you always care for me? Why did you cry and take me in your arms when I told you about my past? Why did you kiss me back?" she shrieked standing up, knocking the chair over.

"I will leave for London after two weeks from now. Think about it, Nikhil. It's about our lives. I will be waiting for your call."

I looked around and found everyone at the restaurant staring at me.

Stunned, I made no attempt to pick the chair up and sagged into my seat. Completely unaware on how to respond anymore, I let her go. I wanted to talk to her and make her understand that I couldn't be with her that way.

Ridhima had become an important person in my life. I had no doubts on that. We had spent so much time together, shared so many things about each other. It was altogether different now.

A couple of minutes later, I got up and started walking towards my car. I was puzzled about how to explain things to her. Maybe giving her space was the right thing to do.

♋

At home, with arms and legs spread on the bed, I continued staring at the ceiling. My mind was too busy contemplating my thoughts and my rusty feelings. I wanted Ridhima to stay with me as she was such a wonderful friend. But of course, not at the cost of her dream and also making her stay would open a door of possibility in her mind that one day I would love her back. I couldn't be so selfish.

I wanted to think about Shanaya and wanted to know what she still meant to me. I extended my hand to grab my phone. Impatiently I tapped my fingers and opened my mailbox. A smile ran over my lips as I saw an email from Shanaya and opened it. She had written a poem:

Every day I am quivering in pain, it's getting difficult day by day
Life has never been so cruel and strange, and I blame my mysterious fate
One moment it's all shimmering, bright and it's shadowy another
Your love is the only thing that keeps me going,
I have a feeling, tell me that's not right
I want you to stay, as I can't let you go away

When things are terrible, deviously strange
I am losing myself because I am burning in pain,
When I travel down memory lane, it's the gratifying memories of your love that makes me stay,
You promised to love me for life and beyond
I promise things will be better this time,
I have a feeling, tell me that's not right
I want you to stay, I can't let you go away

My heart shrieks in pain,
And everyone is turning away, family and my friends,
But I can still take hold of myself from drowning if you are there,
And now as you are perplexed, it torments my brain, seizes my blood and its veins.
The prayers we said aren't going away
I have a feeling, tell me that's not right
I want you to stay, as I can't let you go away

When I flash forward, I see you breathing next to me again
God is never unfaithful, just keep some faith
Forgive me for one last time
As life does always change, nothing is perpetual, but our love
Don't leave me here alone, as you are the only reason I exhale
I promise you I will do everything it takes; you know my heart is in the right place
I can't bear to lose you my darling, don't make my flesh crawl again
I have a feeling, tell me that's not right
Please, I beg you to stay, I can't let you go away.

As I read the last line, tears fell on my cheeks. Every word reflected the pain she had been carrying since so long. It was more than ten months already since our break-up and the rage I had towards her was deeply buried under the sea.

One thing that concerned me the most was something she had written. Friends and family turning away! What did that mean? And how could she know that I was somehow perplexed? Did she see me in the restaurant with Ridhima or did she hear everything? Whatever she meant, my heart was clear now that I couldn't love anyone except Shanaya and I had to let Ridhima go. God knew that I wanted to get back together with her, but only if I could convince myself that she would not repeat what she did.

Recalling the night before the break-up, when I was satisfied with my life as I had my soul mate on my side, was a healing medicine to my profound invisible wounds. Apart from feeling helpless for myself, I was in a dilemma whether this was the dead end or there would be a new light of hope for a new beginning. Was that it or I would have someone in my life who I could love again or maybe trust again? I questioned myself as I turned around on my bed. Life is so cruel. First, it tempts you with things you tend to like and love and then it takes it all away. First Shanaya and now Ridhima – everyone would be taken away from me. I was disappointed.

♋

"I love you," I said, tasting the eight-letter word over my tongue, as I kept my hands on her back, her body rested extravagantly over mine. It was a perfect afternoon at the beach; the sun was immaculately shining in the faithful sky. Once again, I stared deep into the eyes of the love of my life – Shanaya. Within days, my life had changed and I was dragged into paradise. Her face was all I ever wanted to see for the rest of my life. A voice from inside told me that this is what you call heaven.

We were sunbathing, feasting our eyes on the spectacular scenery, and enjoying the moment of togetherness with her head on my chest. I held her hands so snugly that even a tornado couldn't liberate her grip from mine. I glanced around and saw white and grey seagulls flying over the waves.

The sea, massive and amaranthine, rested peacefully under the sun as far as one could see.

Sea waves motioning to and fro like a pendulum were drenching the sand around me, leaving it wet. The humming of the sea was like a chorus of a song playing again and again. Perhaps a love song, sung by every drop of the sea to the sand begging for love and to bond everlastingly. I felt like nature was singing the background music for me while I pressed my lips on hers. She tasted like a divine drink that nourished every part of my body.

"God has given us another chance to love each other for life and beyond," I whispered in her ear.

A smile swept on her face. Her cheeks as red as blood, her eyes manifesting her love for me gazing intensely into my soul through my eyes, and then she said, "If only I could rip my heart and show you how much I love you."

Today in this bright sunlight, she was looking like an angel in her yellow sarong wrapped gracefully around her trim waist. God! She was so gorgeous! My subconscious squealed at me. I gazed towards the sky saying thank you to heaven.

I clutched her in my arms tightly. Her breath fell over my naked chest and once again my entire world was wrapped around me. I was the happiest person on earth.

After a few seconds, when I was still thanking my fate, for giving me back my love, I heard birds screaming for help. I heard the turbulence coming from the sea. Shanaya was no longer in my arms now.

As fast as lightning, I opened my eyes and saw the sun vanishing and found Shanaya running towards the deep sea. Her eyes were swollen, her body felt weak and tears squirted from her eyes. I glanced at her, wanting to know why she was going away. I felt suffocated, desiccated, my heart hammering, my body clutching in pain.

I shouted frantically as I got up from the spot and ran towards her, "Wait! Wait, don't go again! Please!"

She kept walking inside the deep waters. Only her body above the waist could be seen.

I shouted again, "Shanaya! Shanaya, no! I am coming with you!"

And she screamed, "I know you want to be with Ridhima now. You can never forgive me, Nikhil. I am going away for forever."

"No, please wait. I forgive you, I am sorry. You promised me that you will never do something like that."

"You also promised me to love me for life and beyond. Bye, Nikhil," she smiled and disappeared into the sea. I continued running into the water till the water took me fully into its depths. I shouted again, "No! Shanaya!" My legs were cold and I couldn't move.

I felt something was forcing me to stay where I was. I was repelled from going forward. The more I tried, the more I was hurt.

"God! I can't let Shanaya drown, please don't do this to me. I can't live without her. I will take her back, but don't take her away from me!" I cried.

I knew nobody would help me in this situation and I had only two options: either to get up and save her or cry for the rest of my life. Once again, I took a deep breath and with full force I pushed my chest upwards and a painful, remorseful scream sneaked past my throat. Shanaya!

Panicked, I threw my arms around and my hands hurt. It was getting dark, too dark to see.

My eyes opened wide in a flash as I jumped from my bed. I looked around and saw the sunlight streaking into my room from a window over my bed and settling down on the floor. The mirror in front of me showed horror plastered on my face. Damn! Thank god! It was just a nightmare.

I shook my head and folded my hands, gazing towards heaven. "Thank you, god! Please never let anything happen to Shanaya. Give all my happiness to her," I prayed from the bottom of my heart.

My hands shook as I wondered whether she was fine or not. "I have to meet her today," I said out loud this time.

"God! I beg you. Please don't let anything happen to her. She is my life, I love her; don't take her away from me," I muttered.

I searched for my phone on my bed impatiently, but failed to find it. Immediately I stood up and looked around. "There it is." I saw it on the floor beside my bed. I bent down and picked it up. My hand was infinitely quick this time.

Shanaya, are you fine? Please reply fast, I had texted.

Time passed by; my heart beat faster every second. Every second felt like the passing of a lifetime. I groaned inside. I could feel the horror latched onto every cell of my body. Impatient, I started pacing about my room.

A silent prayer travelled from my heart to the heavens for her well-being.

Finally, I decided to call her. What if she didn't pick the call? My hands trembled at the thought. Typing her number at a rapid pace, I pressed the phone to my ear.

Tring tring.

The tone felt crisp, loud and clear. I forced myself to be patient. Another ring passed by, but she didn't pick up. My brain screamed in torture. Apparently, the nightmare was turning to be true. I closed my eyes and flashed them open as the nightmare played again in front of my eyes. I bit my lower lip in fear and my hands shivered continuously.

I couldn't wait and thought of calling her mother now. But then, by god's grace, I heard something that had always stopped my heart from beating. I stood rooted to the spot and wished to dance on the moon at that moment.

"Nikhil...," she said; I took a breath of relief. It was Shanaya. God! I owe everything to you. Thank you! I said silently.

"Shanaya?"

"Yes, Nikhil. What happened?"

I couldn't express my happiness to anyone at that point in time. Silently, I sat on the corner of my bed. Closing my eyes, I imagined her smiling in my mind's studio.

"I am sorry to call you like this; I had a very bad dream," I confessed.

"I am fine. I am here talking to you." Her voice felt like the harmony of angels.

"Can we meet?" I asked desperately, with my fingers curling into a fist, shaking, wanting her to say yes.

"You want to meet me?" She sounded amazed. "Where?"

"Outside your college? We can sit in that coffee place," I suggested.

"Sure." Her reply was quick and her voice was a melody to my ears.

Happiness lurked on my face and I felt my heart beating outside my chest.

"Get ready, bye," I responded, and hung up.

As I got up from my bed, I rushed towards the bathroom for a quick shower. It had been a week since Ridhima had proposed. Self-loathing was at its peak. It was so frustrating that I couldn't move on in my life. I had two people in my life who loved me, but I had become the unfortunate soul who found it difficult to choose between them. I had always thought of love to be a divine and sacred entity, but today, I had second thoughts.

In the past one year, I had never cared whether she was alive or dead although I never stopped loving her. I hated my guts at that moment. "You are the most selfish man on this planet, Nikhil," I alleged as I stood in front of the mirror in the bathroom.

It felt so strange to be meeting her after so many months. I couldn't imagine what she looked like except the mental image that I had buried deep down in my heart. I just hoped that I was ready to meet her.

♋

For the first time in the last one year, I was not late; in fact, I was before time. I entered the café pulling the glass door on the first floor and walked down to the last table in the open area.

I sat down on the chair.

At eleven in the morning on a weekday, the café was as silent as a grave apart from the occasional sound of birds chirping. I gazed around and observed a few staff members.

The staff had lined up wooden tables one after the other and decorated the open area beautifully with potted plants that had lovely, colourful flowers which I guessed were carnations.

My eyes spotted the menu kept at the corner of the table. Bored, I picked it up and started surfing. Seconds later, I heard someone pulling the chair just opposite me.

Dazed, I raised my head and found Shanaya staring at me.

My mouth curved into a smile and before I knew it, it faded. At one moment, my heart exploded with joy and in the next second, it got depressed. My breath ceased for a couple of seconds and my jaw twisted. 'Nikhil, it's all because of you,' I claimed. My eyes blazed with hatred.

Shanaya looked as sad as a sunless sea in her casual white T-shirt and blue jeans. Her face had lost its youth. Her eyes felt like they were singing a mourning tune, as if everything was dying inside her. Her body had weakened as if a devil had sucked out all her happiness and left her with a shattered soul and a hollow skeleton.

Who was that soul-sucking devil? I wondered. And I knew it was nobody else but me. It was evident that she had not been eating well for a very long time.

The more I looked at her, the more my blood flared. I couldn't look at her anymore. She looked completely different from what I had seen every day in my mind. 'This is not Shanaya; the Shanaya I know is very brave and beautiful.' I shook my head regretfully.

She smiled, but the moment my eyes trapped hers, she looked away.

We probably sat there reading each other's minds for a long time when I finally decided to break the ice.

"Hi, how are you?"

She took a moment to collect her words and snorted, "I am okay."

As the seconds passed by, I cursed myself repeatedly. I felt ashamed for not caring for her, for never checking on her or replying to her messages. 'How could you be so selfish, Nikhil?' My mind kept shouting repeatedly. Things happen, but life doesn't end. No one is perfect. All that is important in this world is to learn from your mistakes, I meditated on and on.

Her gaze wavered; she couldn't bring herself to look at me, which made me feel even worse.

"Shanaya, I can't tell you how blessed I am feeling right now, that you are healthy, sitting with me. Please forgive me for my behaviour earlier, forgive me for never taking your calls, forgive me for never caring for you during our break-up."

Her mouth had formed a question mark as she heard my apology. She blinked twice and kept her hands on the table.

"Nikhil, I did something ugly. I had to eat dirt. You don't have to apologize to me."

"I don't want to listen about the past, please forgive me," I pleaded.

"No. I am sorry, but I can't do that." She gave a dismissive wave of her hand. "Please don't make me feel bad, you didn't do anything wrong," she retorted.

I decided to take care of her from now on. I glanced at her once again. I sat baffled, words failing to come to me easily. Apart from the huge bag of guilt on my head, my mind constantly tried to tell something was missing. Did I still love her the way I used to? Would I be able to trust her again? I wondered, scratching my head. There was something very different. I felt sceptical about my feelings today as if I had loved a different girl all this time. I wanted to be sure and decided to take my time before coming up with a conclusion.

I picked up the menu and offered it to her.

"What will you have, Shanaya?" I asked.

"Nothing. I had my breakfast," she responded, looking down at her bare hands.

During our time together, she never had breakfast. It was evident that she was lying.

"Don't lie to me. It's just eleven and you never eat anything for breakfast except for the half cup of morning coffee with a couple of spoons of sugar," I said confidently, crossing my arms over my chest.

She drew closer, her gaze hurt as it penetrated through me. I felt helpless being exposed. Tears shimmered in her eyes.

"You still remember? God! I messed up the best thing that happened to me." She shook her head and her long straight hair swayed back and forth.

"Nikhil, please forgive me. I am very sorry. I know I did something very bad, but what is left with me, if not this? I don't think the punishment fits the crime here. Am I gonna cry for the rest of my life? I must not live any longer than," she said, losing the battle with her tears and they soon flooded on her cheeks.

Immediately I pulled my chair closer to her and wiped her tears with my hands.

"Shanaya, look at me. And don't you dare cry in front of me. You know I can't see you crying." My voice was imposing as I held her face with my hands.

"I forgive you. We will be friends now."

Recognition dawned on my face as I heard those words coming out of my mouth. The nightmare I had in the morning had changed my mind. The fear of losing her for a lifetime made me realize how much I still loved her.

Yes, I had forgiven her seeing the big picture of life. We are humans and we do make mistakes, and she did it too. Life never ends at one thing.

Her eyes glittered with happiness.

"I will be anything you want me to be, Nikhil. You know what, even if you decide to never give me another chance, I will still love you and will wait for you until the last day of my life."

"Shanaya, let's bury the hatchet. Let me order some French fries for you. From now on, you cannot be this thin. I won't let you be this way. The older version of Shanaya was more beautiful."

Then something amazing happened, her soft lips stretched into the most beautiful smile. Wow! I never thought a smile could have so much power. I was happy as a lark. She pressed her hand against mine. I trembled the moment our skin made a contact.

I waved towards the attendant turning my face. In a second, with a smile on her face, the girl in a red apron rushed towards us.

"French fries and a couple of cold coffees for me and my friend."

I said 'my friend' deliberately, to make her more comfortable.

"Sure," she replied, nodding.

"So, what are you doing these days?" I enquired.

"I am working in an internet marketing startup company."

"Oh really, that's impressive," I replied, happy with her accomplishments.

"You know, I have emailed you everything every day about what I did or what happened to me in these months. I had always kept you posted." She wrapped a curl on her finger.

"I am sorry, but I was too furious at you until today, so I paid no attention to your emails." I said even though I had read a few of her emails.

"I have learnt to drive too," she revealed.

"Ahh! Liar," I said as she was always afraid when I asked her to learn driving.

"Nikhil, seriously."

"Seriously!" I blinked in amazement and continued. "That's really great."

"I did everything in these months which you asked me to do earlier. I took my career seriously, I worked hard for this job, I learnt to drive, and I have transformed myself from a short-tempered whining person to a calm, optimistic learner. All through the months of separation from you, I kept a level head."

My mouth was a hard-line. At that moment, I wanted to hug her and praise her for her accomplishments.

"I cannot be prouder of you than I am right now since you have turned over a new leaf, Shanaya," I said.

"Thank you." She smiled.

I took the fries and the cold coffee and pushed it towards her. I picked up the ketchup bottle, squeezed it gently and poured it on Shanaya's plate, making a smiley.

"Here we go!" My face radiated different colours of happiness. She took a sip, and seemed to be collecting her words before she asked, "What are you doing these days?"

"Still working with dad," I replied, "But, it's not turning to be good these days."

"What happened?" she raised her chin, her eyes brimming with concern.

"With a global plummet in prices, we are incurring losses. So, temporarily, we have slowed down. It feels as if everything is falling apart," I retorted.

"Nikhil, just hang on. I am sure you will get the best out of it. Nothing is permanent in life, time will change, things will get better. How do we embrace and cherish the good times if we don't experience the bad?" She wrapped her hand around mine. Her touch made a pandemonium in my head. I felt my pulse rising.

If anybody else on this planet had said what she just said, it would have meant nothing to me, but this time I was optimistic about it. My heart always believed everything that came out of her mouth.

"Thanks for saying that. It means a lot." I drew my hand and took a portion of fries on my plate and began eating.

"Nikhil, you know what, one day, I was crying in my room when my mother entered and asked me the reason for crying out that loud. I told her everything, Nikhil, and at first, she got angry and said distasteful things to me and then after a few hours, she came into my room and consoled me." Her expressions hardened as if I had touched a nerve. Unwillingly, I loomed closer to the table.

"Then?" I asked tapping my fingers against my coffee.

Shanaya shook her head and continued. "She asked me what I wanted in life and I told her that I just want Nikhil to be back with me. She understood my love and has supported me in every way since then."

"I never knew that your mother would be so supportive about this," I said in disbelief.

"Believe it or not, but she has changed a lot."

"Hmm. But Shanaya, you should not wait for me. I cannot trust anyone in my life now. I am damaged beyond repair."

"And that's all because of me. I am really sorry, Nikhil." She looked away.

"Don't be, it's okay. Life moves on."

"I have to go home now," I said taking the last sip of my delicious coffee.

"Sure." She nodded.

We were walking towards our cars when she asked, "Can I take you for a short drive, please? If you are not getting late."

"Okay," I nodded.

I sat in the passenger seat of her car. She buckled up her seat belt.

"You should also put on your seat belt as I am not the experienced one here," she said teasingly.

"I think I should," I smirked, looking at her.

She started the ignition and pressed her foot on the accelerator.

"Don't be scared, I care for you more than I do for myself. You are in safe hands," she said looking towards me.

"Please drive slowly and eyes on the road," I begged with my voice high.

"I just don't believe it!" she announced.

"What? Brakes are working, right?" I asked as fear rained on my face, drenching my mind with negative thoughts.

"Yes, they are working, but I can't believe that you are sitting beside me and I am taking you out for a drive," she said as she changed the gear.

"Oh, you almost gave me a panic attack."

After few minutes of her roller coaster drive, she stopped the car outside the café. I smiled.

"What? You didn't like my driving?" she rolled her eyes at me, throwing an arched eyebrow.

"I liked it, but I was scared. You are a little rash."

"Okay. I will work on it."

"I will be leaving now. I have to go with my father for some work, goodbye," I said while gazing at her face.

"Okay." She nodded. I pulled the handle of the door and was about to get out when she asked.

"Can I hug you once, Nikhil?"

I turned my head towards her and smiled. My mind and body got excited.

Unconsciously, my body slanted towards her. She opened her arms wide and clasped me in her grip. Her warm breath on my shoulder sent goose bumps down every inch of the skin on my body. Seconds later, I found my arms on her back, wrapping her against my chest.

I closed my eyes and ran my hand through her soft silky brown hair. The feel of her body soothed me more than I expected. My world had stopped. It felt warm and right. I had a feeling that something would change for good. Holy crap! My head twisted. Butterflies fluttered in my nervous stomach. I took a deep breath, grasping her aroma from her body.

I was sure that if I stayed for another second in her arms, I might have a breakdown. Immediately, I drew away from her, gently slackening my grip and stepped out. I smiled back at her and waved goodbye.

She waved back and screamed, "Will you pick up my calls from now on?"

"Every time," I replied smiling, and her face once again glowed like it used to once upon a time. An inevitable rush stroked my nervous system, and I wanted to wrap my arms around her again, but I knew I couldn't. All I could do was to come out of the rush of the feelings that were stacking up in my head.

I turned around as she left.

"She is the most beautiful girl alive on this planet," I heard the words coming out of my mouth.

"You love her buddy!" My subconscious yelled at me inducing yet another batch of goose bumps. Damn! My feelings came back running from some secret space.

I couldn't believe what just happened with me. Within a period of a couple of hours, I had a change of heart. I waited at the spot stabilizing myself from the suddenly erupted volcano of my feelings for her. As I walked towards my car, her beautiful face again flickered in my mind's eye. I opened my car and sat inside with my eyebrows snapped together.

Holy shit! I loved her so much. I wished if someone could calm me down. The feeling was quite overwhelming. I had never experienced such a thing before. I wanted to be strong and convince myself to not get back with her, but some parts of my body did not support me at all. My heart shrieked at me to get back with her while my head persistently warned me not to.

Then, a thought knocked over my head. That unfaithful night played on my mind. My muscles scrunched and a wave travelled through my body, causing me excruciating pain.

God! What am I doing? I don't want to feel that again. Happy thoughts! Happy thoughts! I begged.

Taking charge of the steering wheel, I started driving back home. My mind constantly thought about her; her glowing face came repeatedly in front of my eyes, which brought a smile on my face after almost every ten seconds. Damn! I was blushing. God! Thank you! I croaked. Then my heart kicked in, contributing to the vivid memory of our first kiss when I bent down on one knee and proposed to her while I prayed for her to say yes. And then when she kissed me, those butterflies that tormented my stomach with excitement and anxiety, I almost relived that moment, the moment which seemed like the best thing at one point in time.

Even though I never felt anything for Ridhima, but after seeing Shanaya today, I realized that it would have been a heinous crime if I would have given it a thought. My heart only had a place for Shanaya, even if it meant spending my entire life alone without her, but with the memories of our good times.

♋

The day had finally arrived. Ridhima was leaving for London.

I flipped and tossed my phone in my hand, wondering how to say goodbye. I uncrossed my leg and leaned back in my chair. It was sure that she would be a ton hurt. But sometimes in life, the right thing is the hardest thing to do.

Still nervous, I dialled her number. Even after typing her number on the screen, I was in two minds about calling her, but accidentally I pressed the green call button on my screen.

"Hi," she murmured.

I was nervous and remained silent.

"Nikhil, I can hear you breathing."

"Hi, Ridhima. How are you?"

"I am good. I waited for your call for a week. So, I had to pack up my stuff. Not everyone can have what one wants in life, right?"

She was definitely agitated. I hoped that she wouldn't start hating me.

"I am sorry Ridhima. I didn't want to hurt you, but the truth is I still love Shanaya."

"Nikhil, it's okay, don't feel bad. Love cannot be compelled."

"Can we please meet before you go?"

"No, Nikhil, don't make it difficult for me. I can't say goodbye to you. I just can't."

"I don't know what to say... I am sorry."

"Nikhil if I ask you to do something, will you do it?"

"Yes, please!"

She paused for a couple of seconds and said, "You must forgive Shanaya and try to get back with her. I love you with all my heart and I want your happiness, even if it is not with me."

There was some part of me that wanted to tell her that I had met Shanaya.

"You know I met Shanaya a few days back."

"You did what? Are you guys back together?" Her voice was curious.

"No, we are not getting back, but I've decided to be friends with her."

"Hmm. Like this has ever worked out between any two ex-lovers," she replied sarcastically. "Anyway, I will still be there for you whenever you need me. I am just a phone call away."

"Bye, Ridhima. I hope we will be friends forever."

"Yes, we will be friends."

As she disconnected the phone, I felt bad that after so long, when I finally made a good friend, she would be going away. Even if Shanaya and I would get back together anytime in the future, I didn't want to lose a friend like her.

♋

Can we meet tomorrow? I texted Shanaya as I sat down on the bed.

Damn! I cursed myself for sending her the text. You should control yourself, Nikhil! My subconscious barked at me.

A week had passed since we last met. Sleep had been like a friend who never visited. I missed Shanaya badly. She remained all over my head and I couldn't work, eat, or go out. It was like falling for her all over again. The spark which we shared before, had returned. Apparently, not thinking about her was the most difficult task to do throughout the day.

Every day in the last week, my mind and my heart fought like two lawyers in a courtroom, arguing and discussing the pros and cons of getting back with her.

But today, the discussion was going off limits.

And then I thought, what could go wrong in meeting her once again? On any other occasion, my brain would have pointed out plenty of reasons why I should not meet her, but today, it had given up.

I was in the middle of giving my heart a merry go round tour by imagining the good times I had spent with Shanaya before my phone vibrated. I checked and saw Shanaya's text.

Sure, I would love that.

Her reply tempted an ocean wide smile on my face. Abruptly I typed back.

Will be waiting at 1 o clock, Italiano Restaurant.

♋

"Shanaya and I can be friends," I said convincing myself with my hand on the entrance door of the restaurant. The day had been perfect up to now. Firstly, I had the best night's sleep in the last one year. Secondly, I got up with Shanaya's melodic voice just like the old days. It felt as if all my dreams had come true. Motivated to look good in front of her, I wore the blue shirt she had gifted me a couple of years back on my birthday.

I walked inside the restaurant adjusting the collar. My legs stopped walking the moment my eyes found Shanaya sitting at the very first table. Her ethnic attire completely blew my mind, my jaw gaped. She looked exceptionally gorgeous in her black suit. Her face dazzled when her eyes met mine.

I strolled towards the table and sat opposite to her while I extended my hand for a handshake.

"Hi." Our hands met and her soft skin sent jitters all over my body.

"Hey," she replied as her lips widened.

I gawked at her mountain brown eyes; for a change, they were vivacious and bubbly. She put her head down in response to my unwavering gaze. But I felt helpless; her presence left me breathless. Almighty! I love her so much.

"You look so beautiful in Indian attire, Shanaya."

"Thank you very much," she replied looking back at me, raising her head with a smile originating from her extended lips. Her smile made me feel worth living. God! My sun rises and sets with her.

"Is that the same shirt I had given you on your birthday?" she asked pointing a finger at me.

"Yes," I nodded.

She continued staring at me and smiled as if enjoying a private joke.

"What?" I asked curiously tilting my head.

"Nothing. I can't tell you how much it means to me that you are wearing this shirt today. I was afraid that you might have thrown away my gifts."

Although many times out of anger this thought did come across my mind, it always felt awfully painful.

"It's just a nice shirt," I shrugged. "You are forgetting, Shanaya, I am a baniya," I pointed out making double inverted commas with my hands.

"Ha-Ha. I can never forget that," she replied laughing, her head shaking.

"How have you been?"

"I am good. My life is perfect with you in it. Once again, I am sorry, Nikhil, for hurting you." She apologized sadly, looking down at her knotted fingers.

"Shanaya, let's not talk about it. We are friends now, remember?"

"Yeah, I am sorry."

We sat quietly in our chairs, stealing glances at each other. Shanaya certainly had something running in her mind as she continued tapping her fingers on the table and looked away. I wanted to ask her what was going on her mind, but for some reason I wanted her to initiate the conversation.

"Nikhil, if you don't mind, can I ask you something?" Her lips curled inwardly and she looked anxious.

"Umm, finally. Shoot!"

She cleared her throat and said, "I don't know whether I should ask or for that matter whether I can."

"Shanaya, you can ask me anything," I said softly, keeping my hand over hers on the table.

"Do you have a girlfriend?" she asked squaring her shoulders, looking deep into my eyes.

My eyebrow rose as I gazed at her and drew my hand from hers. Her expressions dulled and she looked down.

"Girlfriend. Umm. I don't think so," I smirked teasing her. "I am single, Shanaya."

She took a deep breath and her lips stretched into a smile and it seemed like a load had lifted off her chest.

"What about that girl? Ahh... wait... Ridhima, is it?" she asked massaging her chin with her fingers.

I frowned wondering how she knew about Ridhima.

"I am sorry, do you know her?"

"Umm... I saw a couple of pictures of you and Varun with two girls on Facebook, and in one picture you were holding her hand."

"I did? I don't remember at all," I said, perplexed and continued. "Yeah, Ridhima and Sia. We met them in a club a few months ago and we four have become good friends." I was still thinking how much she had noticed.

"Anyway, you know what, finally Varun is dating Sia."

"Wow! Really? That is just awesome."

"But sadly, Ridhima went to the UK for studies last week." My eyes drooped. "You know what, she did propose to me a few weeks ago," I confessed massaging my chin.

Her head jerked. "Then? You guys dated?" She frowned breaking out in a cold sweat.

I took the liberty to remain silent as I surreptitiously watched the curiosity banking in her eyes.

"Nikhil?" Her eyes widened.

"Like you gave me a choice."

"What?" she inched closer, eyes fixed on me.

"I have always loved you Shanaya."'

"Really?" Her eyes were shining with hope.

"You don't believe me?" I asked.

"No, I do believe you, sorry." Shanaya shook her head."

During lunch, I told her everything about my friendship with Ridhima. She also told me about her job and her colleagues. Soon after, we left the place and went for a short drive. The anger that I had been carrying along with me had secretly vanished after the beautiful day we spent together. All I could think about was how happy I become whenever she gets around me. As they say 'you never forget your first love', I was sure that I could never stop loving Shanaya. Till the time my heart would beat, it would beat for her.

I parked my car outside the restaurant after the drive. There was absolute silence in the car and I could hear us breathing. I gazed at her again; she appeared to have been lost in her thoughts which gave me some time to just stare at her. Damn! I have missed her so much. Why did we break up? We were so good together.

The nightmare which I saw a couple of weeks before had sucked out all the grudges I was holding inside my heart for Shanaya. The only challenge left for me was to take her back in my life. So what if she cheated on me? No one is perfect, everyone makes mistakes, the point is to not repeat it. If I replayed every moment I had spent with her, the only thing I found was happiness.

Nikhil! She was the one who made you cry for such a long period and broke your heart. My brain barged in and barked at me loud and clear. For once, I wanted to take a decision for my life, for once I wanted to choose what my heart really wanted. My heart once again thought of our beautiful time together. Her smile, her voice, her touch meant the world to me. The first thing that I ever see when I close my eyes was her.

No relationship is perfect. Things turn ugly sometimes, way more than anybody would have ever imagined. They say 'if you truly love somebody, you will forgive that person, no matter what, and there is no love without forgiveness', I wanted to forgive her. Life is short and unpredictable. What is more important is to live and cherish the moments happily with the person you love.

With guns and swords, my heart and consciousness battled for justice and then finally my heart won and I decided to forgive her. After all, she had been always the one for me – my love, my soul mate, my everything. Life without her was like the earth without an atmosphere, a river without water, clouds without dust and the sea without life.

Instantly, I had an urge to kiss her. I moved my head closer to her. She sat frozen in her seat. Without wasting another second, I gently leaned in and kissed Shanaya's warm, delicious lips. They drew apart and her breath shook. My tongue entered her moist mouth. I felt a sparkle, a tormented shiver flew in my blood stream, and I pulled my body away from her in reflex, leaving her suddenly. She frowned and gave me an astounded look. And then I held her face with my hands and pulled her into a passionate kiss. It wasn't long when my hands went around her back, feeling every inch of it. The kiss was immortal. Her lips felt the same as they used to. I closed my eyes and enjoyed the tour in heaven.

Angels flew over my head. I heard the nightingale singing loudly. My life wrapped around my body. Within a second, my life was perfect and flawless again.

Never in these months was my body so satiated. My heart was joyful, soaking in her affection, my blood blazed into my veins; every tiny part of my body thanked me for forgiving her.

"You are mine. I love you," I whispered.

Her body trembled as she put her arms around me. I could literally feel her body muscles squashing and soon, she started crying boisterously.

"I was so so alone!" she stammered keeping her head on my right shoulder.

"I am really sorry. Please forgive me and take me back. My life has no meaning if you are not a part of it. I promise you, I will always love you and will never hurt you again," she begged as we parted.

She blinked and tears dropped down onto her cheeks from her eyelids. My heart sank in the ocean of sadness.

"I had no one to share what I was going through, Nikhil; my friends were of no help, they went away when I needed them the most. I could not share anything with my brother. I felt like a fish out of water. At least you have your sister with you to support you," she said staring down at the floor, continuously avoiding eye contact.

"My life became stagnant since the day you left me. Although it was entirely my mistake. But I am a human being, didn't I deserve a second chance, and please I beg you to forgive me. Don't make me suffer throughout my life, I have waited for so long for you. Please, I beg you!" she went on.

"Shanaya, I forgive you, you are mine now."

She raised her head, inched closer and held my face between her hands.

"Seriously? Will you take me back now? Will you love me again?" Her eyes sparkled with happiness.

"Yes."

She cried harder. "Nikhil, please! Make me yours again; I want to feel your love again."

In the next second, she held me in her warm, comforting, loving arms. "I will never let you go now."

"I can't see you cry, stop it now, please!" I ordered.

I thrust her away from me, wiped her tears with my hands, and then clutched her in my arms again.

"Just remember one thing; you are not allowed to cry for the rest of your life. Deal?"

"Deal," she giggled and brushed her lips against mine.

"I promise, Nikhil. I will never cry again. I promise I will never ever hurt you and I will fill your life with love and happiness."